THE DOOMSDAY CLOCK WAS RUNNING—
POWERED BY NUCLEAR FUEL

The Roberts were the only ones to realize what was happening. They knew the effects of nuclear power better than the rest.

They had learned about it from their children, some with deformed bodies, others with strangely altered minds . . . from the animals around them, gentle creatures turned into killers, tiny species grown giant . . . from the monstrous shapes of the new plant life and the poisonous effects of what used to be food.

The Roberts knew what the Normals refused to hear . . . what the Power Companies that controlled America refused to admit . . . what nothing less than a desperate rising in rebellion could hope to avert . . .

The world was about to run out of choices and time— and its last chance for survival lay in the seemingly powerless hands of those who wore—

THE ORANGE R

THE ORANGE R
by John Clagett

AN AUTHORS GUILD BACKINPRINT.COM EDITION

The Orange R

AN AUTHORS GUILD BACKINPRINT.COM EDITION

Published by iUniverse.com, Inc.

For information address:
iUniverse.com, Inc.
620 North 48th Street, Suite 201
Lincoln, NE 68504-3467
www.iuniverse.com

Originally published by Popular Library

ISBN: 0-595-00296-X

Printed in the United States of America

Foreword

Though industrial mankind is tampering ignorantly
with the basic forces of creation and destruction,
with things completely beyond the empirical knowledge of man, this book is wild, exaggerated, base-
less, illogical, unscientific, and unlikely.
   I hope.

Chapter One /

ROBERT COUNTRY

Powerman Second Class Kirk Patrick was finishing off the last half hour of his night watch at the board. He wasn't very sleepy, even though he hadn't had his usual evening nap before coming on watch. He had been to a party, and the bittersweet thoughts about the party and Anne had stayed warm in his mind all night. He was alert in his comfortable, molded chair before the board, the vital and essential indicators clear and calming in his mind. Years of training in alertness had banished inattention. Casualness or slackness in a duty officer was unthinkable when an error on his part might bring about a major catastrophe. Kirk could watch the dials of his board for hours on end; when all was wholly normal his mind might be anywhere. But the slightest change in a reading acted upon him as a call sign does upon an expert radio operator. It closed a switch in his brain and his total attention was focused blindingly on the board. He had been trained in this technique during his four years at the Power Academy. By the time he was a Powercadet First Class, he had been required to sit at a board for as much as seventy-two hours at a stretch; if he failed to note and act upon the faintest change in the board during that period, he had failed the test. Too many failures could bilge a cadet, even in his first-class year.

The room was spotless, antiseptic, and cool; it contained only his chair and the board. Beyond the door, marked on the outer side with its crossed lightning flashes, was the main control room and the watch crew of watermen, rodmen, and technicians. No sound of the life there penetrated into the watch room, no one entered unless summoned, with three exceptions: the powerchief, the duty officer's relief, or the senior technician in the control room, if the "dead man's switch" were activated. Kirk wore sensors as a part of his crisp white-and-gold uniform; changes in his heartbeat, respiration, anything that indicated a change in his physical condition, anything out of the ordinary, sounded alarms in several places in the plant, and he would be checked at once by the senior control room technician and relieved by the powerchief of the plant if necessary. Junior officers joked about the device, remarking that it should be called the "sleeping man's switch." If a duty officer fell asleep, even for a moment, the alarm would sound—and the culprit would wish he hadn't.

Anne in the moonlight, the little lake, the night breeze that moved her hair and that he couldn't feel, the single enormous white star shining in the dark blue night sky above the mountain peak. He remembered the—

A bell sounded three notes. The clock before Kirk showed 0645 hours. That would be his relief; Frank Owen always relieved right on the minute.

Kirk pressed a switch on the chair arm and Owen came in.

"Welcome, stranger," Kirk said. "How's the weather outside?"

"Early," said Owen. "Beyond that, I think I saw some blue sky through the lake haze. You sound chipper. Want to stay a while longer?"

"Hah! Fat chance. Let's see. MW fifteen hundred; reactors B and C on the line, A warming up for the morning peak. Rods 37.4; water temperature three-fifty on the nose. No problems. Take a scan, Frank."

Standing by the chair, Owen studied the board carefully for a time. Then he nodded.

"Ready to relieve you, sir." The crisp formality in his voice indicated the seriousness of this statement.

"Sir, the board is yours." Kirk's tone matched the formality of Owen's. He stood up. Directly before the chair was a plate with two locks. A key with a dependent chain hanging from it was inserted in one. Owen took a similar key from around his neck and inserted it in the open keyhole. Kirk withdrew his own key and hung it around his neck, then gave Owen a smart military salute, returned by the latter with equal smartness. Then both relaxed.

"You got the sack, brother," Kirk said happily. "I got places to go and things to see."

"I got it, bub. Now don't tantalize me with your childish plans. If you feel like getting peeled in tennis this afternoon about four, I'll see you at the courts."

Kirk yawned elaborately, indicating how very good bed was going to feel. He wondered, a bit wryly, what Frank would say if he knew that the heavy date was to visit the Waybury Elementary School, second grade. Didn't sound exciting, but it was tremendously so for Kirk. Anne Martin taught that grade, and she had invited him to visit her there this morning.

He usually went straight to the wardroom for breakfast after coming off watch, but this time he headed for his room, hung his gold-and-white uniform carefully so that it would do for another watch, pressed the button that turned opaque the glass wall of his room, which fronted on trees, a large boulder, ferns, and the forest floor. Another button brought his bed, freshly made, sliding out of the wall. He got into it, said: "Wake me at 0900. Lights out." The lights dimmed out, and he was almost instantly asleep.

Music came on at nine o'clock, waking Kirk. He rolled from the bed and it slid back into the wall. He showered, dressed in civilian clothes, got some brunch in the wardroom, and was on his way.

The elementary school was a long, low building of brick, planted with birch and maple trees. Inside, he found himself in a noisy hum of children. He was directed down the corridor, where he found and knocked on a door marked: *Second Grade—Miss Martin*. He heard voices, and knocked again. The door opened to reveal a little girl facing him. Her blonde hair was in pigtails and her blue eyes were sparkling with delight, and there was something reminiscent of childhood reading, something pixieish, in her appearance.

"This is the second grade, with Miss Martin

teaching. Good morning, sir." She giggled at her own formality.

"I'm Mr. Patrick." Kirk bowed gravely. "Will you tell Miss Martin that I'm here?"

"She knows it's you," she said. "Come on in."

Passing her, Kirk realized why the little girl reminded him of childhood imaginings, for her ears were pointed on top and perhaps an inch higher than they should have been. On her it was charming, not grotesque. One wall of the sunny room was of glass, and through it he could see a playground, a meadow, woods, and the mountains beyond. Anne came to him smiling.

"So glad to see you, Kirk. But I am afraid you must be sleepy. When I invited you to come this morning, I simply didn't think about the night watch you're on. You deserve a reward for getting up so early in order to come to see us. Children," she said. "Children!"

"Good morning, Mr. Kirk Patrick," the class said, then burst into a song of welcome.

Kirk was delighted. He hadn't had much contact with children, and there was something about this group that appealed to him. Probably it was Anne, he thought; she seemed to have infected all of them with her sunny and warm personality. They went on with their lessons while Kirk sat quietly at the side of the room and watched. Anne told him that they were in the midst of their reading period and would have to finish it even though they had a guest, after which they would have a recess. Kirk watched the children. At first, pleased and happy at the sight of Anne, he didn't notice some things about them. They seemed to be perfectly normal, happy-looking children, intensely serious in their concentration on the reading Anne was requesting them to do. As he watched, he began to see others who stood out, not in any major way, but who seemed to have something vaguely different about them, an eye a little bit out of place, one ear larger than the other, no eyebrows, and the sunny, golden-haired little girl with her pixie ears. Careful inspection showed him a girl with an artificial arm. Further search revealed two, possibly three, others with artificial arms. The few Norm children in the class wore their suits and helmets, otherwise each seeming exactly like any other happy, busy child. Kirk thought that there was something about childhood that could redeem the human race, if only society could refrain from spoiling its shining warmth and sincerity. He smiled wryly at the thought; after all, mankind had been thrown from the Garden, exiled from innocence, after eating the fruit of the tree of the knowledge of good and evil.

A boy stood up to read, and Kirk felt his throat constrict as he looked at him. He had heard of such things, but it was quite different actually to see a good-looking, cheerful small boy standing on one leg—not one leg gone, just one leg. Like a mermaid without scales, and her tail replaced by a single leg and foot. On that foot the boy balanced steadily alongside his desk, reading clearly and well.

"Thank you, William," Anne said. "That's very good. Now, Adam. How about you?"

The child who stood up was quite close to Kirk, and the latter saw him clearly and shuddered again. This boy was perfectly formed and with the largest eyes Kirk had ever seen, but there was something grotesque about him. The head was larger than it should have been. Not large enough to be *really* grotesque, but certainly noticeably too large for his body. The boy stood silently and his smile made Kirk feel like Herod.

Gently Anne said, "Will you read for us, Adam?" The boy smiled at her, the smile of unspoiled childhood, and shook his head. He said nothing.

"Please, Adam," Anne said. "You see, we have a guest today, Mr. Patrick."

The clear blue eyes and face full of innocence, questioning, and something more—was it compassion?—were turned toward Kirk. Adam smiled again.

"Aren't you ready yet, Adam?" Anne asked. "I would like to hear you read today."

The boy shook his head and bowed it, seeming sad, the smile gone.

"That's all right, Adam." Infinite sadness was in Anne's voice. "You may sit down. Perhaps you will be ready to read to us tomorrow."

The children were putting away books, erasing the blackboard, and getting ready to go out for recess. Kirk felt sick. Anne came toward him carrying a book, and their eyes met. For the first time hers seemed hostile, and Kirk understood. He could understand that any woman who loved children and who was here with these children who had to carry the burden of their deformities all their lives could not help but feel angry at someone who, however innocently, represented the forces that had brought this about. Not simply at Anne's blankness and coldness, not simply at the children he had seen, not simply at George Sneck sitting comfortably and at ease within the dome insulated from all this, not even at the power structures in New York and major cities across the nation, not at any one of these, but at all together, Kirk felt an immense rage, as well as sadness for the futility and blindness of men. He could not hold back the tears that came to his eyes. Crying! he thought. Within his helmet, he could not wipe away the tears, and he blinked to clear his eyes. Anne saw, and the coldness left her face and she smiled at him, reaching out with both her hands to squeeze his within the plastic gloves. The orange R glowed on her left hand.

"I'm so sorry about these children, Anne."

"Are you? Well, these are nothing. They are all right, they will do very well. They have more courage than any adult. The other children think nothing of it, really. The real Deforms are bad! They are in a special school where they are trying"—the bitterness returned to her voice—"to equip them for some sort of life. I guess it's lucky that the really bad ones always die right after birth—ones with a chin resting on the pelvis, an extra arm, no eyes, no legs, or with bad hearts, or lungs that don't work. They don't live, thank God!" Tears came to her eyes.

What a pair of lovers we are! Kirk thought. I have never touched her, she has never touched me. The suit is always between us. We stand here, both crying within; how can there be room for love and happiness in a world where things like this exist? But there had to be love and happiness. There must be times when one could be joyful, or else the world would be filled, not simply with struggling and unhappy people, but with insane people. And that would be the worst of all.

"Your Adam," Kirk said.

"The boy with the big head. Thoughtless people call them the Big Heads. There are a few of them here."

"He must be rather retarded. Doesn't he talk at all?"

"*Retarded!*" Anne said scornfully. "You sound like some of the people I know. They are not retarded, Kirk. I have one in my room and there are two in the first grade. I know of four or five younger ones in town, probably more. Adam is the oldest one that I know. They are slow to learn to talk, and afterwards they talk only a little. Adam says very little and he won't take his turn at reading. He just smiles. I've heard him talk to the other children, though, and sometimes he talks to me. Usually he simply says, 'I'm not ready yet, Miss Martin.'"

"Sometimes the late bloomers are very fine, you know," Kirk said.

"Yes. There's something I feel about him when I'm with him. In fact I sometimes feel a little afraid of him, almost. And that is so silly. He's such a *sweet* person."

"That shows clearly in his face."

"I'm happy you said that." Anne smiled. "You know, when you spend a little time with Adam or any of the other children with big heads, soon the head doesn't look big at all. The other children's heads look too small."

Someone knocked at the door. "It must be the

nurse, Miss Martin!" somebody shouted. There was a race for the door, and in came a beaming lady dressed in white with a black bag in her hand.

"It's the nurse!" said the children. "It's time for shots!"

"Yes, children, this is your shot day. Line up. Miss Martin, will you stamp the books while I give the shots, please?"

"Of course. Excuse me, Kirk. This will take only a few minutes and then the children will go out and play."

There was a brief flurry in the room as the children dug out their shot books. Most of them had the books hanging around their necks on a thin chain. Kirk, of course, knew about the shots. They had been discovered just as radiation was growing intense, the result of a years-long crash governmental research program. All Roberts received the vaccine regularly, frequency varying according to the amount of radiation registered in the patient's body. With these shots, a Robert could live in health. Missing two of them brought illness; missing three or four brought death. The vaccine was manufactured under government contract in Normal country, where proper facilities were abundant, and was distributed free to all who needed it. Kirk knew that its manufacture required extremely high temperatures and an enormous amount of electrical power, and that the vaccine could be stored for only a short time. The life of every Robert depended upon the supply not being interrupted. These children around him were chained to the shots for life, were dependent upon them for life itself. Oh, damn it all! Kirk cried silently. God, what have we done? Now the room was full of laughter, with one small boy jumping up and down in delight.

"Oh, Miss Jones, Miss Jones, you took the wrong arm again!"

"The wrong arm again!" children shouted throughout the room.

"Oh, dear," said the nurse. "Can you imagine that? Here I am trying to give Tommy a shot in his artificial arm. Isn't that silly? Let's have the other arm, then." Laughter shook the place. Kirk found himself laughing too, and then he found himself—was it crying? Boy, what a sad sack he was becoming!

When the shots were done and the notations made in the books, the children bustled into sweaters and jackets and poured out of the room through a door leading directly onto the playground. Suddenly the room was empty and Kirk and Anne were there alone. She was putting on a light coat to go out and watch the children.

"Oh, God," Kirk said. "Anne, I feel so sorry! You know, dear, if there were anything in the world I could do to undo what has been done, I'd sure take a whack at it."

"I believe you, Kirk, and so would I. But don't feel too badly. Look out the window and watch them. I saw you looking at William, the boy with one leg—well, you watch him. They're playing tag out there now. See the one who's the hardest of all to catch, the one who can catch any of them?"

Kirk looked out of the window. The one-legged boy was bounding across the grass in great leaps, his flexible, broad-shouldered, symmetrical body swaying in a marvelous kind of balance. As he watched he saw that William had advantages; he could turn, literally, on a dime, and change directions so fast that no child could come close to him when chasing him and no child could escape him.

"He's the champion tag player in our room," Anne said, "and believe it or not, his favorite game is basketball. He's going to make a great basketball player someday. He has the most marvelous balance. He's like a tightrope walker, and when he falls, he falls loosely and is back on his foot again at once. They're all like that, they accept their problems, their deformities. Deformities! I hate that word! They accept their problems and they fight them. And they'll win, oh, they'll win."

Recess was still in progress when Kirk left the school. He drove down Court Street, around the green by the inn, and parked in front of the Post Office. Across the broad street stood a gray stone Episcopal church. On this day at this hour it would be empty. Kirk walked across the street and went into the cool interior. He sat in a pew and bowed his head on his arm. The sickness, the anger, the warning that clutched within him had not released its hold on his heart. Kirk looked up at the altar and the flowers. He knelt. He could feel the tears streaming down his face. He cried, "Oh, God, oh, God, forgive us! Forgive us all!" He knelt there a while, feeling a kind of acceptance, a kind of serenity moving over him. The tears ceased. He had never cried so much before. He felt as if he had passed through some bitter and major experience, and he felt a loosening of tension, a relaxation.

"Thank you, Sir." he said.

18

He drove through the lovely September day back to Lake Dunmore and the glittering bubble of the plant. He went into his room, got out his bottle of Canadian Mist, and had four drinks. Then he went to bed and to sleep. By dinner time the alcohol would be gone from his system and he wouldn't need it again. He'd be sober and rested when he took his seat before the board in the control room. He slept and dreamed; he was Adam and William and the other children too, but the dreams weren't nightmares because they smiled at him and because Anne Martin was there.

*　*　*

It had all begun only a few weeks before Kirk's visit to the elementary school when Bill Knock, a gangling young man with a friendly face, came into the small room they shared at the Darien relay station.

"Big news, buddy," he said, grinning. "The printer just carried a message for you from downtown. The powermaster of VPC wants to see you tomorrow morning at 10:30. Can you make it?"

Kirk grinned back and said, "Yes, I think I can spare the powermaster a little of my time. Was there anything in the message that showed what I'm in for?"

"Nope. It just said for you to report to the Powermaster, VPC, 10:30 tomorrow morning, September first. Whatcha been doing you shouldn't have been doing?"

"My conscience is clear—well, pretty clear. Actually, I think it may be a transfer. I haven't served in Robert country yet."

"Probably right, damn it. I get a roommate broken in properly and they get rid of him. Good luck, son. I hope you get a good station, not in the Antarctic. Boy! That place is cold!"

Kirk was only faintly uneasy. If powermasters were irritated at you they didn't bother to talk; they simply said *Chop off his head!* and that was it. He was alert on his afternoon watch. The control board was automatic, but it was necessary to have a trained human being standing ready for any emergency that might come. It wasn't like a watch on a nuclear board, of course, but still a large portion of the power delivered to the city of New York from the Northeast came through here, and you were alert every moment when you were sitting in that comfortable duty officer's chair before it.

Kirk Patrick had determined early in life to be a powerman. He had taken his B.S. degree in power from the University of Arizona with marks high enough to gain him entrance to the Power Academy. He graduated in the upper half of his class as a Powerman Fourth Class, with an unlimited basic license. He had been working for VPC ever since; it was not one of the biggest, but it was in a solid financial position with a long list of producing plants and a wide market for its power. Thus far, all his jobs had been in Normal country. He had a notion that things were going to change now.

Kirk slept well when he went off watch, for he didn't think any of his minor sins had been serious enough to have reached the upper office. He break-fasted with Bill Knock, who teased him consider-ably. This was reassuring; Bill would not have done so had he believed Kirk to be in trouble.

"I got a great idea!" Bill exclaimed, beaming over his bacon and eggs—deradded, since even VPC wasn't about to waste real fresh eggs on its junior officers' mess. "When the powermaster gives you a chance, you tell him you've got a revolution-ary idea that will revolutionize the power industry. Clean, no radioactivity, everlasting . . ." Kirk found the laughter forming already. ". . . solar en-ergy!" Kirk and Bill Knock both burst out in roars of laughter. Kirk laughed so hard that he almost choked on a bite of bacon that he had already swallowed.

"Sure," he gasped. "I'll tell him! Solar pow—" He was off again, laughter overcoming him.

"What the devil are you two jackasses braying at?" demanded a Powerman First who had been quietly reading a newspaper at a nearby table. "You're disturbing the joint."

"Oh, Kirk here is going to tell the Powermaster, VPC, all about—solar power." Knock lost control again. The First Class threw back his head and laughed as well. He wiped the tears from his eyes and said, still chuckling, "You jerks stop that dirty talk. I got to get out of here, and I can't eat when I'm laughing."

Kirk took out his handkerchief and wiped his eyes. As he did so, a small voice somewhere within asked him why he had laughed like that. Well, damn it all, solar power was funny, it had always been funny, ever since a bunch of crackpots back in the twentieth century had tried to beat down nuclear power with it. It had become a joke long ago. Nightclub comics used it, comic books had their most futile characters involved with it. Punk Year at the Academy had been full of it; the endless skits and jokes that Punks had had to learn about solar energy were often obscene, usually bawdy, and occasionally funny. The power companies still attacked it—sometimes Kirk wondered why. He recalled a recent 3-D TV commercial that showed a man frozen in a block of ice. Powermen chipped him loose with old-fashioned ice picks and asked him what was the matter. "I heated my house with solar power," he said, teeth chattering. The whole lounge had burst into raucous laughter at that one.

Bill Knock, seeing Kirk silent and thinking him to be worried, took a moment for his own thoughts. He would be sorry to see this boy leave Darien. He was a quiet, good humored sort of guy, easy to get along with, good in his work, perfectly dependable. Ready to take a shift for a friend anytime. He was a little old-fashioned and conservative maybe, bashful—he didn't like to screw in public, or even in company with a friend, but all the same he was amusing, a good talker. Kirk was sandy haired, freckle-faced, about five feet eight inches tall, weighed about 160 to 165, and was in top shape. A good tennis player. They had some good games that summer. Some of Kirk's hobbies were a little unusual since he came from the southwest where there was still a good deal of open country. He liked to hunt and fish, and climb mountains, and ski. Bill Knock liked to ski, too, but in the East all the skiing was done in Robert country, and he hated to wear a suit.

After breakfast, Bill drove his friend to the station. As they drove through the quiet streets he asked for the third time, "Have you made your will yet, Kirk? Might need it, you never know. And say, don't forget that solar power."

He nearly ran off the road laughing, and Kirk was laughing too hard to be scared. Also, he was wondering if they would make the station on time. He had decided not to take his car into town, to ride the monorail instead. Traffic in New York was rough, even though nonessential automobile traffic had been banned. Kirk's license plates, marked with the crossed lightning emblem of a powerman, enabled him to drive anywhere, but he still didn't like fighting traffic. The windows of Bill's Chevelectric were down, and always in the background there muttered the distant surflike sound of an air plant. A string of them lay all around New York, and successive strings of them ran across the countryside. Air was forced through the air plants and cleaned of radioactivity.

They arrived as the train pulled in. Kirk got aboard and took the first seat available, just as the train pulled smoothly away. No need to buy a newspaper, for he would be at Grand Central in a few minutes. Once this would have been a depressing scene through which he traveled, with slums, garbage, factories, a smutty sky, dirty water when water was visible, and an endless scab of decayed-looking structures spread on each side of the railroad tracks. Now it was green everywhere, interspersed with a forest of spaced tall buildings.

Around each building was a green park. There were many factories, for this was an industrial area, but they were surrounded by grass and trees. A slogan one caught occasionally on the large billboards along the way, A GREEN LEAF IS LIFE, showed that the function of the tree in preserving oxygen and in cleaning the air had been fully realized. Anything that helped keep air normal now was an essential for the civilization that existed within it. The sky was a clear, deep blue, and a few white clouds floated in it. Everything was sharply cut in the distance. The closer apartments were blurred with the motion of the train, but on the distant ones Kirk could see the rows of balconies, one outside each apartment, and the green things growing on them that made green strips across the varicolored buildings.

Kirk arrived at Grand Central on time and moved from the train into a jostling mass of people that carried the individual along with its own weight. New York still drew to its immense number of offices, restaurants, shops, theaters, museums, sports centers, and galleries a seething tide of humanity that flowed twice a day. The sky overhead was dotted at this hour of the morning with helicopters. They were allowed only in minimum numbers, reserved for senior executives and high-ranking government officials. Kirk hurried across 43rd Street, on to Madison, across Madison to Fifth Avenue, and stopped and looked at his watch—bumped into from all sides as he did so—no one said, "Excuse me." This was New York, of course, and one had to expect it. He looked up and down the avenue, feeling the little glow of excitement that always struck him even now when he stood on this street in New York City. After all, he was a country boy from Tucson, which had barely more than a million people. Kirk pressed the button. On the tiny screen, figures and letters appeared: *0903, Thursday, September 1, Sunrise 0543, Sunset 1931.* He took his finger off the button. Had he not done so, the clearly traced letters and figures would have been followed by the weather forecast and radiation count. He had plenty of time, so he decided to walk downtown.

VPC was not a pretentious company. It had its main offices in one of the smaller structures—the Empire State Building still carried a certain feeling of conservative solidity, though it was barely a hundred stories tall. It had the swank of an old-fashioned gentlemen's club. Kirk saw the sign turn to WALK and surged across the avenue with a hundred others. Forty-second Street hadn't changed much. He walked past the New York Public Library and looked down the canyon of high buildings. The sidewalks were covered with rushing people. The sex shops were open, doing a great business. Every block or so there was a sex theater, advertising the latest movie star appearing in the latest sensational films in three-dimensional color. Kirk hadn't much interest in these places. He didn't care much for spectator sports himself, he liked those things that one participated in. The dance, as Lydia called it, hunting, fishing, skiing, swimming. Someday maybe he'd be high enough in VPC to have a house, not an apartment, and a swimming pool. Such things were allowed once you got past a certain stage. He walked slowly down Fifth Avenue, a moving mite caught in the bottom of a tremendous canyon. Restrictions or no restrictions, the avenue was full of traffic—one way downtown. The cross streets were choked. He sauntered along, whistling. He was young. One did not see the powermaster every day of the week or every month of the year, or every year.

The buildings were tall, and the authorities had required open space around each, so that grass, flowers and trees grew between them. Looking down the avenue Kirk could see for miles, with every building sharp cut, distinct; no soot or dirt blew in the wind. Garden-club litter baskets studded the avenue, and cleaning crews emptied them several times a day. No one had to work very hard in this culture, but everyone had something to do. Education on television, in books, and in schools had allowed people to realize that such jobs were as honorable as any others. It was a matter of necessity to keep cities clean; they had become such vast hives of humanity that order and regulation had become absolutely essential. Of course, all this was paid for in the loss of individual freedom. In some things one didn't have very much choice. Such things as where one lived. Such things as one's job. Such things as when one could get married, and even the decision as to when one could have a child.

Since Radiation, unradiated clean land was at such a premium that no structure was allowed any more on open land anywhere. High taxes imposed on land that did not grow grass or trees or food had stopped the outward surge of the cities. By persuasion, by making the inner city a beautiful place with all kinds of diversions and activities for people, the government had forced people back into the city and higher into the sky within the cities. There had been no choice, Kirk knew and he proudly felt himself a functioning part of the machinery that kept this vast structure, and a hundred others, going. You were safe on the streets of New York now; they were well policed by excellent helicopter police service, patrol cars, and foot patrolmen. The drug problem had almost been solved. You saw an occasional drug addict moving along, eyes dull, shoulders hunched, sometimes almost skipping in the warmth of a good high. Drugs were furnished to addicts, on the condition that they accept treatment, and drug-control treatments were successful in most cases. The race problem had been solved, too, or at least ameliorated so that no longer were the streets dangerous. All of the old slums had been razed. Instead, the tall apartment houses, well built, comfortable, and with all conveniences, were spread all over Manhattan island. After the riots, all minority groups had been dispersed throughout the entire city, so there were no concentrations of race. There was no discrimination in jobs. Educational opportunities were the same for everyone. And the lack of individual freedom was the same for everyone.

Kirk was pretty close to his destination now. He entered the nearest park, sat on a bench, and waited, relaxed and calm, or almost calm. A group of sightseeing Roberts came into the area, laughing and talking gayly. Kirk could see through the transparent helmet that one of them was a lovely girl with bronze-gold hair and a lively, attractive face. Nicely dressed, too. The tough, impermeable substance of her suit was no hindrance to vision, and he could see that her clothes were nicely chosen, colorful and gay. She wasn't dressed like a country girl at all, though most Roberts were country people. Kirk caught her eyes, which were blue and pleasant. He stood up, lifted his hat, and bowed. He was not a Robertist. Back in college he had known a number of Roberts. Indeed, some of his best friends in those days had been Roberts; he still remembered them with pleasure.

Now it was ten o'clock. The meeting was set for 10:30, but he knew it was a good idea to arrive early when you were coming to a meeting with the powermaster. There would be preliminaries and people to meet. You didn't just go directly into the office of a powermaster and say "Well, here I am, sir."

The VPC offices began on the 20th floor, with reception on the 25th. Kirk stepped from the elevator and walked across the room with the deep rugs to the brown desk, behind which sat a pretty girl who greeted him with a smile that promised while remaining impersonal and cool.

"May I help you?" she said.

"Yes, please, my name is Patrick, Kirk Patrick. I have an appointment with the Powermaster, VPC."

She consulted a list and said, "Oh, yes. First, Mr. Patrick, you must have a medical examination. I'll have someone take you to the doctor." She pushed a button, said something, and in a moment another girl appeared and smiled at Kirk. She led him down the corridor and indicated a door.

"They will call me when he's through," she said.

"And I will take you,"—she consulted a slip—"to the powermaster for Vermont."

"Vermont," said Kirk. Then it *was* a tour in Robert country—in Vermont. That could be very interesting.

The doctor was brisk, as all doctors were. He seemed to give one a clear understanding that he was one of those upon whom the burden of the world rested. Not too much of a pose, Kirk knew. There still were a tremendous number of old medical problems to be handled, plus many new ones. Kirk removed his clothing and lay down on the table. The nurse attached the sensors deftly and quickly, the machine began to purr, and lights blinked. The doctor watched the various dials and indicators carefully. When the test was over he examined Kirk's left hand thoroughly under a special light, then nodded. He had him exercise. He listened to his heart again.

"The machines are good," the doctor said, "but I still think there's a place in medicine for good old-fashioned physical contact and intuition. See," he said, "I even use a stethoscope." He did so.

Kirk was told to dress again, and then was handed a card bearing his medical report.

"You're in fine shape, young man," the doctor said. "You're as clean as anyone I've seen in a long time. You have spent a great deal of your time in clean Normal country, correct?"

"Yes, sir, I have been fortunate that way. I'm from Tucson, sir."

"I see. I understand that you are going to Robert country. This is our routine medical inspection for people so ordered. I would advise you, Mr. Patrick, to limit your budget time to an hour a week, and I would also advise you not to take more than fifteen minutes in any one day. Watch your readings carefully. We don't want to lose a good clean man. Why, you should be good for a half dozen or more Robert country appointments without approaching the danger level, if you're careful. Good day."

The Powermaster, Vermont, was an older man, rather brusque, puffing on a large cigar. His office was ostentatious, his receptionist was pretty, his secretary handsome. His voice was unnecessarily loud as he spoke into his desk intercom. The pretty face of his receptionist appeared there, vanished, and then returned and said something to the powermaster. He snapped the set off and stood up.

"Mr. Bright will see you now, Patrick," he said. Mr. Bright was the powermaster for the entire VPC operation. Kirk knew that he was considered to be one of the most promising senior executives in the organization, with a possibility of becoming powermaster for all of the northeast area, a position of vast importance. Kirk felt a few butterflies in his stomach at the thought of meeting a man who had gone so far and done so much.

The powermaster's office was a corner one with windows on two sides. Kirk got a glimpse of the river far away, and of the spires of New Jersey, with the palisades beyond. The man at the desk smiled pleasantly as he stood up, looking to be about forty years old. His face was round; it looked young except for the lines of character. He was dressed conservatively, his hair trimmed in the senior executive fashion, and a handkerchief was visible in the left-breast pocket of his suit. He was polished. He was firm. He was the organization man. Kirk felt a little awed with him.

Bright said, "Kirk Patrick. Yes, you're the young man who is going into Robert country. That's all right, George, I'll take over now. Thank you very much for bringing Kirk in." The Powermaster, Vermont, left with the receptionist.

"Sit down, son," said Mr. Bright. He leaned far back in his beautiful chair and put his feet up on his beautiful desk. "Pardon my informality," he said, "but when one gets a moment or two to relax, it's nice to take advantage of them. I envy you this new step in your career. You, by now, should know that you're being ordered to Vermont, Station V7. It's on a nice lake in the mountains, quite close to a pleasant little town called Waybury."

"Waybury," said Kirk. "Isn't there a college there?"

"Yes. As a matter of fact, young man, I once knew that area quite well. It's pleasant country with some unusually nice Roberts."

Kirk knew that the Powermaster, Vermont, would not have used that tone in speaking of Roberts. He would not have said *nice* Roberts, or, had he done so, he would have used a tone that would have made it an expression of contempt. This man seemed to mean it. Normally, you didn't speak to a powermaster, certainly not this high a powermaster, without being spoken to, but Bright had seemed to suggest that informal conversation would be in order.

"I know someone teaching at Waybury College," Kirk said.

"Good," said Mr. Bright. "That will give you an

in with the college community. As I say, young man, I rather envy you. There are restrictions, of course. You will probably find a little difficulty in becoming accustomed to wearing the suit at all times, but over all, Robert-country duty is a good one for a young man, for it makes him understand the responsibility that we power people have. We have changed the world, so we must take care of the world, and power is the one essential."

"Yes, sir," said Kirk. He had heard this before, and he felt it to be true. One always realized that from the reaction of people to the identification card of a powerman, for they realized that their very lives depended on the power.

"You are being promoted to Powerman Second Class," Bright went on. "You've done some good work, and you can consider this a step up in your work with our company. As is usual before being dispatched into Robert country, you have a week's home leave."

"Thank you, sir."

"Very well, Mr. Patrick, I guess that's all. Good luck." Bright reached out a hand. Kirk mastered the impulse to wipe his on his pants leg, and then clasped hands. The door opened and the receptionist appeared.

"This way, sir," she said.

Kirk was home in Tucson for dinner that night. His father was a successful market research man, and the Patrick family home was large and comfortable, an apartment on the tenth floor with an unusually large balcony. It was located on the outskirts of Tucson. The skyscrapers of the city stretched away on one side, and on the other were the lush green irrigated fields of Arizona. This was Normal country, and none of the land was allowed to go to waste.

Mr. Patrick was pleased about Kirk's new assignment. He had always told his son that he must expect to spend a considerable portion of his time in Robert country, and, as he now declared again and again, there was no place in Robert country that would be a better place to go than Waybury, Vermont. He had spent skiing weekends, fishing trips, and an occasional vacation at Waybury, visiting an old friend who taught at Waybury College, Professor John Martin.

"I'll write John at once that you're coming, son," his father said. "You'll enjoy meeting him, and you'll like the people up there."

"Thanks, Dad. I know somebody who teaches in the college, too, so I'll be well equipped with introductions."

His mother was worried. She tried to hide it, but every now and then she'd break in with: "Oh, Kirk, do be careful. I do want you to stay clean. Your father and I would love to have a grandchild someday."

"Now, Mother," Mr. Patrick said. "Kirk is well trained, and the equipment is excellent. He is in no more danger in Robert than in Normal country, if he keeps his head and follows directions."

"That's right, Dad. They never let us forget. This morning the doctor said that I was remarkably clean, and that I could have as much as an hour a week in budget time."

"Good, son. Spend it wisely. Take it when you're out in the woods. There's nothing I know of that smells like the woods in the mountains of Vermont."

Kirk enjoyed the dinner very much. He had been eating New York food, mostly deradded, for so long that to taste this Normal food from Normal country farmland was simply wonderful. The deradder, although it had undoubtedly saved the race from starvation, did something to the flavor of food. It was never the same after deradiation.

The week in Tucson passed very quickly for Kirk. He did a little mountain climbing. Not the strenuous, sheer rock-wall type, but simply moving by the effort of his own body up and up over the rugged natural structure of the mountains, smelling the smells, seeing the sights, seeing the earth drop below him, little by little, his heart pounding heavily with exertion sometimes, his lungs puffing, natural sweat trickling down his face, the hot sun warming him through, breathing the air, his face free to it, the breeze touching it, thinking of the months to come when very seldom would the open air touch his face. He reached the top of one peak and looked out over the valley. Once it had been desert; now, right up to sheer rock wall the gardens began. It had been done with underground irrigation, water brought all the way down from the Northwest, passing, of course, routine deradiation on the way. Water had performed the old miracle on this land and the rest of the Southwest; the previously driest parts of the United States now provided most of the Normal foods. He sat on the mountain for a long time. The sun began to drop. He was longing to return to the days, forgotten—not just forgotten, lost, impossible forever—when he could have had a cabin in the mountains and passed his life in surroundings like these. He pulled himself from the dream; eventually he would have to live in a city, because in the Normal world there was no other place to live now.

That night Lydia Engels called. She was an old partner of Kirk's, blonde, beautiful, slender, very well exercised, and an artist at the dance. Her choreographer had just presented her with an entirely new routine, and she wondered if Kirk would come partner her for it. Kirk's already sore muscles cried out a protest, but still—the next morning he would leave for New York, and in a few days from thence to Robert country, wrapped in the tough plastic of a suit. He knew there were few Normal girls in Robert country, and of course the Roberts, no matter how attractive, were unthinkable. He said yes.

Lydia was an interior decorator, very successful for one so young, and her apartment was bigger than that of most single people her age. She had two balconies, one living room and bedroom; her living room was a spacious twelve feet square, and the kitchen and bath were modern, sparkling, and well equipped. At the touch of a button, as Kirk well knew, the wall between bedroom and living room rose quietly into the overhead, creating a spacious and luxurious living space, with deep carpets, glass walls opening on a wide view and onto the balcony, and a wide Sturgis-Holcomb airbed. Like floating on a cloud, their advertisements claimed. Not an air mattress; the occupants of the bed were supported on satin over a surface of air; the bed could be made hard or soft at a word, it could massage, it could swing like a hammock, it could—if the mood took the owner—buck like a bronco and be synchronized with anything. It's control console reminded Kirk of a power control board—only smaller. Lydia was not only successful; her wealthy parents gave her an additional allowance so that she had every luxury.

Lydia was beautiful, no doubt about it. She was in a black hostess gown. The fabric over breasts, belly, and mound was like spiderwebs, lending only a dark shadow that increased the effect of white, pink, and curling gold. In a subtly humorous touch, it came up to her throat in a small white ruff. She was perfectly formed. Kirk was glad to see that she wasn't wearing the navel stud her father had given her on her twenty-first birthday; Kirk thought that a diamond there was only gilding the lily.

Kirk hadn't arrived until 9:30—he hadn't been invited for dinner, only the dance—and anyway he had wanted that last nonderadded dinner with his parents.

"So glad you could come, Kirk, dear!" Lydia exclaimed, kissing him. "I do hope you are rested and fresh. This new routine is very exciting. And rather demanding."

"Oh, God," Kirk said. "One of those. Look, darling, I went mountain climbing today. Can't we just screw?"

She pouted and simulated anger. "You *know* that I want to dance, not just"—she hesitated—"screw. And I wish you wouldn't use such vulgar words, I much prefer *dance*. It *is* a dance, you know, and a very artistic one."

"Sorry," Kirk said, with resignation.

"Only savages and Roberts 'screw,' as you term it. For civilized people, it is the greatest of living art forms."

"Yes, dear," Kirk said.

"We'll have a drink first. It's early—why don't you take a refresher? Then I'll have a magnum of nice cold champagne waiting."

"Okay. Maybe that's what I need."

The bath cabinet simply took over. First heat for ten minutes; then an air massage that soothed every sweat-soaked muscle; then an icy shower that revived and reawakened, then a warm and scented shower, then cool again, a deodorant spray, then drying in warm, perfumed air playing gently over his body. He stepped out of the bath and put on a silk robe that Lydia had waiting, held by the mechanical valet. The wall was up when he went out; the champagne waited, encased in ice. Lydia was waiting too.

They drank. "You're ready?" she asked. She touched a console and quiet background music changed to something tense and feverish. "The routine has special music," she said, happily. "Demetry composed it. Now first you . . ."

Every muscle was double sore when Kirk woke up the next morning. And not from the mountain climbing. "Good God," he muttered. "That Demetry must be a cross between a goat and a gymnast." He groaned and got out of bed. "What a routine," he thought as he staggered toward his bath, more than ready for the soothing massage.

* * *

On the morning of his departure from New York, Kirk said his good-byes to his colleagues at the relay station and put his luggage in the back of his Fordelectric. He carried two suits, each still contained in its zippered canvas container, fitted with back straps for convenience in carrying. They were furnished by VPC and were the best that could be found. The good old Vermont Power Corporation took good care of its employees.

Kirk was in no hurry on this drive; he was nervous about going into Robert country, but fascinated over what he would find there. His father had told him a great deal about Vermont, its natural beauty, its streams, lakes, meadows, and mountains. "From what John says in his letters, it hasn't changed much, physically. It has more cows than people again, and furnishes a great deal of milk to New York and Boston."

"I thought the milk would be dirty," Kirk had said. "Doesn't it take radiation awfully easily?"

"Yes, but the deradders work. Thank God for them."

Bill Knock was the only one who came outside to see Kirk off, for a big company was an impersonal kind of thing. Kirk waved at Bill, turned on the ignition key, released the brake, and touched the accelerator. The car moved gently down the winding driveway and through the trees that surrounded the relay station. He was on the Merritt Parkway in five minutes. He drove north on it to the intersection with Route 7. He had decided not to follow the New York Thruway, for he wanted to see all of the country that he could. There was a good deal of traffic, and an occasional town slowed

38

him down. Trees were everywhere; this was an important tree area, carefully tended, carefully supervised, valuable for wood products used so widely in so many things, and also for the broad green leaves. He looked at his map. He would be in Normal country for only a little while longer, because he was coming into the well-watered, less populated areas where the nuclear power plants had first been placed for convenience, cheapness, and access to cooling water. In such areas, since it was already Robert land, more plants were being placed every year to keep up with the increasing demand for power. Kirk didn't drive very fast, so that it took more than an hour and a half before he approached the first warning sign. YOU ARE APPROACHING BORDER COUNTRY, the sign said. YOU ARE APPROACHING BORDER COUNTRY, another sign said. PREPARE TO SEAL, a third sign said. Kirk drove a mile or so farther and pulled into a rest area; he circled down by a small stream that gurgled and splashed over rocks. He looked up at the clear blue sky. There was no trace of smog, for it was gone long ago. No one burned coal or gasoline anymore. One would as soon think of polluting water, or those other things upon which the future of the human race so precariously depended. Kirk got out of the car and let the breeze play over him. He listened to the distant sound of an air plant. He listened to the water. A nuthatch called rather harshly from up in the woods and he lifted his face to the cry, thinking of the fly rod he had in the back of his car. He'd do some fishing while he was in Vermont. Through the pine needles, the sun was warm on his face and the breeze caressed him. He unzipped the canvas pack and got into the suit. The material was perfectly clear, very tough, and quite flexible. It was quite light, and the attached boots were comfortable. He zipped up the airtight zippers. He didn't have to put on the gloves or seal the flexible helmet yet, since his car would be sealed. Nor would he have to put on the air and power pack which furnished the air that one breathed in the suit, passing through the deradder, the cooler, and the cleaner. He got back into his car. He rolled up the windows and pushed the seal button. The red light came on for a moment while the pressure mounted, and then faded away, for the car was now tight.

He drove through the birches around Pittsfield— Robert country now—and across the border. A small sign at the foot of a long hill said WELCOME TO VERMONT. He drove through rural country; the road wound up and over mountains, the valley to his right stretching down with green fields, and then up again to a mountain ridge that already showed some color. Cows grazed in the open meadows. The occasional farms had red barns much bigger than the farmhouses, and children in the yards waved at him as he drove past. There was little traffic. The trains reached everywhere again, as they had many years ago, but he had wanted to have his car with him in Vermont. He glanced at his fuel gauge and remembered that he hadn't filled up for a week or so. Within a mile he pulled into an Exxon station, the bell ringing inside the building as the car went across the pneumatic hose. The middle-aged man who came out wore the green Exxon overalls and cap. He was not wearing a suit, for this was Robert country now. Kirk noticed with a distinct shock the uncovered, open-air-revealed vivid R on the back of the man's left hand, two inches tall, about an inch and a half across, glowing with a vivid, sharp, evil orange.

Chapter Two /

THE KEY

Kirk had a speaker in the side of the car which transmitted his voice through to the outside as if he had simply spoken through an open window. The attendant nodded, took the leads from the pump in one hand, flipped up the access door with the other, fastened the two leads, and pulled the switch. The ampere-hour dial started turning rapidly. Kirk stretched and leaned back, watching the charge needle in his gauge steadily climbing to the right. He took his wallet from the access pocket of his protective suit and took out the credit card. He held it up for the attendant. The man nodded even as he washed the bugs from the windshield. The driver's door had an air lock in it for use when the car was sealed. Kirk pulled back the handle, put the card within the compartment, and shoved the handle through, opening it from the other side as it closed on his. The windshield was clean and Kirk's batteries were charged. The attendant took the card and went inside. He came back shortly with a small square of paper and put paper and card through the lock to Kirk. Kirk checked the number of ampere-hours with the dial on the pump and pressed his thumbprint on the lower-right-hand corner of the piece of paper before passing it back to the attendant. The man smiled and thanked him, his voice as perfectly audible as if the window had been down. Kirk drove off.

He was driving up a mountain valley now, the walls coming slowly toward him. He passed more farms with large red barns and meadows still green. Kirk felt himself to be a country boy. He had been raised much of his life in farm country, and all of these things were of interest to him. A little town, a bigger town—Manchester, rather a handsome place with some fine old buildings and some lovely trees, a good many people moving about. Each, except for the tourists in suits, with the glow of the fluorescent R on the left hand. Already seeing the R had less impact on Kirk, and he figured that within a few days he wouldn't notice it very much at all.

He almost stopped as he went by the Orvis fishing headquarters, for he was a trout fisherman, but he decided that he had better push on for Waybury. He was in Rutland by three o'clock, fought his way through the fair amount of traffic along the one long road with a number of stop lights, and then took off on a road along a mountainside a bit above the valley where Otter Creek wound in the flat, bordered always by its rows of trees. It was a beautiful day and Kirk found himself whistling. Occasionally on the ridges of the hills he could see the square shapes of air plants and hear the distant rush of air, a soothing sound to him. Beyond Brandon he came to an intersection where Route 73 turned off of Route 7 to the right. Silver Lake, Lake Dunmore, the sign said, and to its left a dark sign with orange lettering on metal said: PLANT V7, VPC—TWO MILES. He nodded at it as he went by, for that was the road to his station. He wasn't due to report until the next morning, so he drove on to Waybury. He was eager for the job, but he didn't want to arrive at the end of the day with himself tired and the other people immersed in their routines. Morning was always a better time to hit a new job. Kirk knew he had a good deal to learn about operating an atomic power plant, though of course he had had the basics and the theory, as well as time as a junior assistant officer of the watch at a big board down in New York. All the same, when you began applying these things in a practical way it was a different matter. He'd qualified to stand the board watch unsupervised, and he knew he could handle it. But he still wanted to get the feel of things before he had his first watch.

A little later he was entering Waybury, undistinguished on its southern approaches. There were some magnificent elms left here, but not many; most had gone in the blight until the Harper treatment had been discovered. He rode around the little central green. He saw the Midway Inn, and behind it a parking area surrounded by a motel attachment. The motel had been normalized. Funny how some nut of an artist many years ago had wrapped apartment buildings and hotels in plastic as a work of art, and now it was done as a practical matter. The motel annex was sheeted over with the clear plastic, windows, walls, and all. This meant that the motel unit was completely sealed in, so he could take off his suit and relax. There were only one or two places left in the parking area. Kirk took one of them and turned off the motor. Now was the moment. Heretofore, for most of his life, the Roberts had been those set apart from him and society by their suits. Now he was the one to be set apart from society by his suit, for his protection of course, whereas in the case of the Roberts it was for the protection of the Normal country and the Norms. He had worn suits many times before, but now he was to live in this country for a year. Whenever he was out of his car or normalized living quarters he would have to wear the suit.

Kirk sighed and set about sealing into the suit. The helmet used in temperate Robert country was much more comfortable than the rigid spherical affair of the arctic or jungle. It was made of flexible clear plastic, divided by an airtight zipper parallel to the shoulders. When it was open, the front half hung down on the chest, out of the way; the rear half was down the back like a ski jacket hood, wholly unnoticeable. The tiny microphone and speakers were embedded in the plastic and were no larger or heavier than a dime. Kirk reached behind, brought the back half up over his head, raised the front half, and zipped the helmet almost shut. He slipped the power pack on his belt and plugged it into the suit. He pressed the switch and the pack started pumping cleaned and irradiated air through his helmet. He sealed the helmet zipper, sealing himself off from the world. Pressures were so set that air pressure within the helmet was very slightly above that of the outside air as a protection against leaks; this pressure differential also inflated the flexible helmet just sufficiently to keep

46

it clear of the face. The suit was very comfortable; without the power pack, it weighed barely two pounds. The power pack weighed two more pounds. It was a miracle of functionalism. It cleaned the air Kirk breathed, maintained his suit at a comfortable temperature, and protected him against radiation.

The lobby of the Midway Inn was crowded. The Norms were in their suits with helmets closed, because this main part of the inn was not normalized. The inn was a pleasant colonial structure, and the lobby floorboards were wide and creaked with age. The desk clerk found Kirk's name at once and registered him with a smile. There were several bellboys in sight. Two of them were in suits, except for helmet, which meant they were available to carry baggage into the normalized part of the hotel. At a gesture from the desk clerk, one of them put on gloves, zipped his helmet, and came to Kirk smiling at him through the clear plastic. The helmets did not impede hearing; as a matter of fact, the wearer could turn up the controls and hear sounds that would have been utterly beyond his ability to hear ordinarily. Conversation between people wearing suits, or an unsuited person and a person in a suit, was as effortless and as easy as if the suit had not existed.

"Bags in the car, sir?" the young man said.

"Yes." Kirk followed him out to the parking space, where the bellboy took the one suitcase that Kirk was going to unload for the night. All his luggage utilized a layer of the same insulating material that was in his suit, and was impervious to moderate radiation.

The motel door was an air lock. You opened the outer door and a red light came on. You walked in and closed the outer door; the red light continued to burn until pumps replaced the outer air with clean air. When the red light went off, Kirk and the suited bellboy went into the motel. His room was pretty standard; a wide picture window looked out upon the paved parking place. It was carpeted from wall to wall, there was a 3-D color TV, of course, a double bed with a gadget that jiggled it if you put a silver dollar in the slot, a gleaming bathroom—the works. Kirk tipped the boy and saw the door close behind him with a feeling. for the moment, of intense loneliness. This was the beginning of a new life. Kirk removed his suit and hung it up; he stretched and relaxed, feeling free again. He went down the corridor to the ice machine and filled a plastic bucket with the clean ice. He opened his bottle of Canadian Mist and had a drink. It tasted good and soothed some of the wrinkles from his mind after the changes and adjustments of this day. He knew that a Norm stationed in Robert country had to be careful with booze, because it could become awfully easy to use it too much, to make up for the freedom that one lost in the rather unnatural way of life that the suit demanded.

He had been surprised that the inn was so busy and that there were so many Normal cars parked in the parking area and about the green. "College," the bellboy had told him with a grin. "Waybury College opens this week, and these are parents bringing up their kids. By next week we will be lucky to be half full. Then the foliage season starts, and we get a lot of leaf lookers up here. After that it's pretty dull until hunting season. Deer season brings a few, and then skiing, of course. We have pretty good business. It was a good thing you made reservations, sir, or you never would have gotten in today."

Kirk decided that this was a pleasant time to be coming up here. He was so surrounded by Normal people that he didn't feel at all alien. He thought of the college. Waybury was coeducational—that is, it had both Normal and Robert students. Its faculty was largely Robert, but there also were a number of Normal teachers taking a tour of duty in Robert country. Some of these teachers were very serious people who wanted to try to reduce the wall that was gradually climbing ever higher between the Roberts and the Norms. Others were not good enough for the competition in Normal colleges and universities.

At dinner in the normalized dining room, Kirk had a good meal. One look at the menu told him that the parents who brought their children to Waybury were successful people with good incomes, for there was a fairly good selection of food that had not been deradded. Kirk couldn't afford that kind of luxury himself, as a regular thing, and he took a deradded meal. The steak was good enough and tender, and the coffee, vegetables, and everything were all safe because this was a normalized dining room. But even the Roberts themselves never ate food grown in Robert country without having it deradded first. That deradding process had saved the world, for without it the food supply would not have been adequate for the teeming millions. Technology was not always destructive, Kirk thought. It was technology that had devised the deradding process that had saved humanity.

A rather attractive woman was sitting at a table not too far from Kirk. She wore a sophisticated cocktail dress that was transparent in the chic places. She looked young and had a fine figure. She caught his eye and smiled warmly at him before turning to her own food. Kirk was a little surprised that she wore a cocktail dress up here, for the Roberts were rather conservative and didn't like the revealing aspects of some of the more formal wear of Normal country. Kirk shrugged; he was pretty old-fashioned himself, he guessed.

After dinner, Kirk suited up and went for a walk. He had been told that after a couple of weeks he would no longer even be conscious of having a suit on. As a matter of fact this presented one of the dangers of service in Robert country. More than one Norm on a Robert tour had gotten absentminded and found himself strolling around outside without his suit. If that happened too often, it ended his tour immediately. He was rushed back to Normal country where, after a time, unless the dosage had been too severe, he could be made clean again. But it all added up; if a man had too many of those experiences, that R, which was on everybody's left hand, though perfectly invisible in a Normal, would begin to glow with a little pink in the dark, showing that he had been irrevocably tainted with a certain number of rads. When the R became orange, the man was a Robert. This was one of the occupational hazards of the power business, and it had happened to some.

It wasn't far to the college, and Kirk decided to walk there. He strolled down the little hill, across another green, and over a bridge that looked down on a waterfall with a lovely, wide, swirling pool of water below, the rush of the water over the falls drowning out the sound of the distant air plant. The area about the pool had been made into a park. A drift log was floating around in an endless circle, unable for the moment to break free and drift on down Otter Creek. Kirk decided he'd have to canoe on that water sometime before long, and see what the creek was like. He continued on up a hill, turned left, and stood in the night looking about him at the dormitories with their windows aglow. These must be the freshman dorms, he thought. Beyond a stretch of beautiful green lawn on a hill was a classic revival chapel with a New England steeple above. It was a handsome building and the lighting was very effective. Square stone buildings stood to either side of the chapel itself. Behind the street upon which he stood were other buildings of gray stone, obviously very old. He knew that the college was rather proud of its age. Students were moving across the campus in the soft warm night. Some were talking in little groups, often of Norms and Roberts mixed. The Roberts seemed easy and gay like any young people, standing open to the wind, night, and stars, and Kirk envied them. But he envied them only their freedom; he did not envy them those Rs, which now and then were visible in the dark, if one watched with attention.

His father had told him that the Waybury alums were very loyal supporters of the college. Remembering this college with affection, many of them still sent their children up at least for a year, and some for as many as four. Some of the dormitories had been normalized, with their own normalized dining rooms. Norms had to wear suits to classes, to labs, and for social gatherings. It was a considerable sacrifice, of course, Kirk felt. But he was beginning to believe it was one that was well worthwhile, seeing the obvious friendliness and lack of restraint between the Norms and the Roberts. As his father said, kids are crazy and sometimes there was an accident, but it didn't happen as often as one might think because no one wanted the restrictions of being a Robert. It was almost impossible for a Robert to travel alone, he had to wear a suit when in Normal country, and of course there was the abnormally high incidence of all forms of cancer among the unfortunate Roberts.

Back at the inn, he found his room to be lonely. He was not sleepy, so he went down to the Pine Room for company and a nightcap. He found the lady in black sitting there, and she smiled at him as he came in. He bowed and went to the bar. Shortly afterward she came to him, carrying her own drink, and introduced herself. They talked for a few moments. He could see now, close up, that she was not quite as young as she had looked. There was apparently a fitted transparent girdle beneath the cocktail dress.

"Are you alone?" she asked.

"Yes," he said. "I'm a powerman, stationed at the plant down at Lake Dunmore."

"Then you will be here for quite a while, won't you?"

"Yes, ma'am, at least a year."

"Oh," she said, "it must be dull surrounded by Roberts all the time. I bet it will be a long year, and you look young and healthy."

"Thank you."

"Would you care to dance?" she said, smiling.

The next morning, Kirk couldn't quite figure out why he had said, "No, thank you, I'm rather tired. I think I'll go to bed and sleep." He supposed it was because somehow she, her dress, her invitation, smacked of those crowded streets in New York with their sex shops and shows with their choreographers. It seemed all right there, but up here it was out of place; he had a notion these Vermont Roberts were not like that. He had gone to bed alone and had slept soundly, to awaken to another beautiful day.

After breakfast Kirk checked out and drove south on Route 7. The road on which he turned from the highway wound through woods and past a fish hatchery, a wooded ridge rising to the left. Birds were singing in the trees. He had his suit on so that he didn't worry about having the car sealed. He decided he might as well get used to the suit, and he knew that soon he would take it off inside the station. The road forked and he turned to the right, following the signs. The lake was lovely; he could see the mist rising from the warm water into the cool September air, the mountains behind it high and serene. Power lines cut down the mountain in several places, all converging to the single set of cables coming across the lake, striding across the water on tall steel towers that looked like enormous hunchbacked headless dwarfs, their arms hanging down. He had read a little bit about this plant, and knew that the construction of this power line across the water had been considered a necessity. It had also been expensive. Dunmore was a handsome lake, and the plant had been bitterly resisted by the Roberts who had camps and houses around its edge, but that, of course, had been simply too bad. People could not be allowed to stand in the path of progress. Progress? Survival really, because without the power from the atomic power plants scattered all through Robert country, the endangered areas of Normal country in the United States and Canada would have slowly faded, shrunk, and vanished. The power lines were pretty ugly, but Kirk had gotten so accustomed to them and so convinced of their necessity that much of the time he could look up without seeing them. Even with the power-line scars, the mountains were still majestic, rising into the blue sky covered with trees, except, of course, where the herbicides used by the power company to clear the rights of way had turned everything brown and dead.

To his left was the shining dome of Vermont Plant 7, his home. He turned onto the road and approached it, passing the signs demanding that all who had no official business there stay clear. He drove up to the gate of the dome, stopped, and got out of his car. It was a standard power dome, perhaps two hundred feet high and three hundred yards across. The plastic protective sheeting was rigid and tough enough to support itself, but for safety's sake a few spiderlike steel girders made marks across its clear transparency. Three enormous pipes brought water from the lake, and three more pipes returned the heated water to it through tall cooling towers, where some proportion of the immense quantities of heat were removed. Conditions were such at the moment that there was no fog from these towers, though the slight movement of air above showed where heat was rising.

Kirk walked to the personnel air lock leading into the plant. He would have to identify himself before they would allow his car to enter through the major air lock entrance. The guard was waiting for him. Kirk had his ID card ready, and passed it through the small access lock provided for this purpose. The man studied it a moment, looked at him through the transparent gate, and nodded. A click, a buzz, and the small door opened at Kirk's pull, a red light came on in the little chamber beyond. He closed the door, air pumps sighed, the light went off, and he opened the door and stepped into the dome of the power plant where he would be employed.

"Mr. Patrick," said the guard, smiling, "welcome to Plant V7." He didn't offer to shake hands, since Kirk was still wearing his suit from outside. "You might as well bring your car in," the man said. "I'll have the outer lock gate open in a moment."

Kirk went back through the air lock and a moment later drove his car into the vehicle entrance lock. The gate closed behind him; ten seconds later he drove out onto a graveled drive under the brilliance of the sunlit dome. The plant itself, high, black, and windowless, occupied the central portion of the area; it was at least two hundred feet across and reached nearly to the top of the dome.

Around the edges of the enclosed space were various structures that appeared to be small apartments. Kirk saw a few individual houses, some shops, garages, tennis courts and putting greens, and a swimming pool. The space between the outer buildings and the plant itself was green, with flower beds and clumps of trees. The air was at precisely the most comfortable temperature for the human body. The smell of water from the fountains and the pool, and that of flowers and green growing things, lay in the gently circulating air. Kirk's first stop was the suit room. He removed his suit and helmet, put them on a rack, and went out of the room a free man.

Service in atomic plants was much like duty on atomic submarines. A powerman was restricted in his movements outside of the plant, and in exchange for the loss of liberty, the companies attempted to provide all the amenities and comforts that anyone could reasonably want. Wives who had not yet had their quota of children came up only for short visits with their husbands. Wives who had had their two, and had then been sterilized, as all were, might come up and stay for the entire year's tour. There were not very many of these, however, for most of the technicians and people who worked in the plant were unmarried. A number of Roberts were employed in various capacities, and they were required to wear their suits while within the dome for the protection of the contained environment.

Kirk knew that his first duty was to report to the plant commander. He parked his car before the office building pointed out by the guard and went in.

The secretary was a young Robert girl, nicely dressed beneath her suit; she was pretty too, Kirk noted. He introduced himself, explained why he was there, and listened to the message on the intercom.

"Mr. Sneck will see you immediately," she said with a smile. "This way, please." She knocked at the door, and when a voice boomed, "Come in," she pushed it open.

Kirk went through and the door was closed behind him. The office looked out on the gardens, pool, and fountains. The desk wasn't as big as the powermaster's in New York City, but it was a comfortable and adequate desk with a big chair. Other chairs were about the room, and a low coffee table. A half-open door showed an executive bathroom. On the wall above the desk was, of course, the inevitable framed photograph of Douglas Meredith that was to be found on the wall of the office of every executive of VPC.

George Sneck was a florid man going a little bald on top. He wore his remaining brown hair a little long in the back, reaching down nearly to his collar; it really was a style more suitable to an age younger than his forty-five to fifty. His eyes were a little small for his face, his nose was large, the mouth was small, and there were two chins. He was smiling now as he held out his hand.

"By Meredith, Patrick, I'm glad to see you. We've been shorthanded for the last few days. One of our lads got an extra dose of radiation and had to be returned to New York. You may have heard."

"Yes, sir, they told me something about that, sir."

"Is this your first Robert-country duty?" Sneck

asked, after Kirk had seated himself at the invitation and turned down a cigarette. Clean cigarette, of course.

"Yes, sir," Kirk said.

"And you're how old? Let's see, twenty-eight. By Meredith, sir, if I had my way, no young powerman in this company would serve as many years as you have without a little touch of Robert territory. After all, it's in Robert territory that we have to live, and I must say that I like it. A man can breathe in Robert territory—there aren't so many people around. The dome is a fine place to live, too."

"Yes, sir," Kirk said. He knew that George Sneck was a mustang, an old term that meant one who had come up from the ranks. He had never gotten his degree in power, and he was now about as high as he would ever go in power science, with the rank of powerchief. The company had trained him, as it did many diligent employees of considerable intelligence, so that now he was perfectly capable of handling an atomic power plant. But he would never know the board rooms of power in the big cities. Sneck was wearing the comfortable indoor garb of a man in a dome: light slacks, tennis shoes, and a short-sleeved shirt open at the neck. Kirk could see the matted hair in the V of the open shirt. There was hair on the back of the man's hands, and he wore an old-time RAF moustache.

As a new junior officer just arrived, Kirk was naturally given the night shift, eleven o'clock in the evening to seven in the morning, which he would keep for some time to come. He didn't resent it; he had expected it, for it was customary. He knew that otherwise his time would be free; he could sleep in the evenings and have the mornings and afternoons for outdoors, which he looked forward to intensely. He wondered what the fishing was like in Lake Dunmore. He had never cared very much for night life. And really, in Robert country, there was very little that one could do at night. Perhaps some functions at the college would be fun. Dome parties were arranged from time to time to keep up morale. But the girls at dome parties were always quite few, and always, always, spoken for, except for some of the older ones. Most plant supervisors forbade group dances among personnel, thinking that sometimes it led to hard feelings. Kirk looked across the dome and up at the mountains and the forest, circling blue and hazy all around, and thought that he could take his pleasure there.

He met the personnel officer of the plant. He had lunch, a pleasant meal, all natural food, never deradded, that had been shipped up in sealed freight cars and from thence by sealed truck to the plant. Seven or eight faces got confused with seven or eight names in the usual way. Kirk shook hands all around. Carl Bender, Frank Owen, his wife Mary Owen, Max Orson, visitors from a nearby air plant, and several others. Kirk didn't worry about names too much at the moment. He knew they would all sort themselves out only too well during the year to come.

Kirk liked his quarters. They were on the ground floor, with glass and flowers outside, and a picture window opened in the back through the dome itself to woods, lake, and the mountain. The room was larger than the motel room; it was designed as a comfortable living room with a bed that came out of the wall at command. Another touch of a button could darken all the glass to opaqueness if he wanted to sleep during the daytime, and as a night-shift man he probably would find that necessary. He had his own bathroom, a comfortable chair, a desk. All in all, he was fixed up snug as mice and really thought he was going to enjoy the duty here. Frank and Mary Owen came by in midafternoon, paying a call of courtesy and welcome. Mary was an attractive younger woman, who would be here only for a few months before returning home for safety's sake. They had only the one child, who had been left at home with the grandparents, naturally. Frank was a sunburned, husky-looking young fellow with a smack of out-of-doors about him.

"How's the fishing in the lake, Frank?" Kirk asked.

"Well, it's pretty good. I guess it's not like it used to be, but there are some fine big catfish here."

"Catfish? No trout?"

"Trout? of course not, the water's too warm. Oh, there might be a few brown trout surviving, but not very many. It gets pretty warm for them. As a matter of fact, there are no small-mouthed bass, but there are some good big large-mouthed ones. I caught an old lunker the other day that must have been nine pounds if he was an ounce. Big bass are not very good eating, though. The warm water kind of makes the flesh coarse, I think. Catfish are better."

60

"How about ice fishing?"

"Are you nuts, man? Ice fishing? You don't think this place freezes in winter, do you? There may be a little patch of ice here and there, and sometimes a skim over the top."

"I've heard too many stories about Vermont as it used to be. I forgot what the hell I'm doing. You're right, Frank. Hey, don't tell Sneck about that or he'd probably ship me right back to Normal country."

"He just might," Frank said. "Old Sneck can be pretty tough sometimes."

There was a ceremony before dinner, complete with toasts, and with all the officer personnel of the station present. Kirk was given his key to the board. The key was a symbol of intense personal trust. It would open the door of the central control room, it would turn on the board, and it would allow him access to the destruct mechanism contained there. The control rooms were so arranged that should a Robert come inside and approach the board, the radiation inherent within his bone and muscle would throw a switch and the plant would be destroyed. Not with an atomic explosion, of course, but the delicate control systems, the mechanical marvels of the plant itself, the vigilant computer, all of these things would be ruined. Probably, with the resources in their hands, the Roberts could not put a wrecked plant back into operation. Kirk understood the theoretical necessity for this. He was aware of the growing estrangement between Roberts and Normals, and one couldn't blame the Roberts, really. But all of Normal life, all the future, depended on an uninterrupted, continuous, and increasing flow of power from the nuclear plants. If the Roberts should get control of these plants they might, unless they were better men than Kirk felt himself to be, hold up Normal land. They might even disrupt the flow of power, and all Norm country itself would become Robert country within a matter of years. Therefore, these precautions were taken in every atomic plant.

"Use it, Mr. Patrick," said George Sneck, placing the key in his hands, its link of sinuous chain dangling below it, "use it with honor, with care, and with faithfulness. Congratulations, young man. It's a great thing to have a key to a board."

"Thank you, sir," said Kirk.

The group applauded. The men shook hands with him, the ladies kissed him, and then they had drinks all around. Afterward they went in to dinner.

* * *

Professor John Martin felt old as he sat in the doctor's office, looking at his friend, Dr. Ted Carter.

"So," he said, feeling immensely depressed and frightened, "I've got it, Ted?"

"Yes, John, you have it. The tests are back. There isn't any doubt about it at all."

John Martin heaved a sigh. He felt drained, tired, and irritated at himself because he, a Robert, was devastated within at the news that he had cancer. Pushing sixty as he was, why should he be surprised? Ted was watching his face and reading his thoughts; now he smiled and put a hand on John Martin's.

"Look, you old fud, it's not that bad. Sure a lot of us go of cancer; I guess the death rate is pretty nearly fifty percent now, but other things have eased off and that's one of the reasons the cancer proportion is so high."

"Cheer me up some more," John said, trying to smile.

"I know it's a shock, John, but actually, you know, it's a long way from being the end of the world, even for you." Ted Carter looked down at his own hand, where the orange R glowed. "The radiation to which we have been and are exposed, the number of rads our bodies contain, these make us more susceptible to cancer, but at the same time they control it, or seem to help control it in most cases."

"I'd heard that," John Martin said. "Well, what do I do now?"

"Just exactly what you've always been doing. Come back and see me every three months, and we'll check into how things are going. Here's a prescription, some pills to take. Oh, no, they're not for pain. You're not going to feel anything; as a matter of fact, John, with this type that you have and with it coming on at your age, I guarantee that for the next ten years or so you won't even know that you have it."

"You're just trying to cheer me up."

"Nope, I would say ten or twelve years with no effect at all, except that you take these pills and come for a checkup every three months. After ten years, maybe more, you'll start feeling tireder all the time and less able to do things, which you would anyway since you'll be around seventy then. Maybe there'll be some pain, but new drugs we have control it absolutely, so you'll feel nothing. When the time comes that you do begin to feel pain we can't control, when life doesn't seem worthwhile any longer, when you feel really sick, then comes the Anteroom."

"The Anteroom. The very sight of that place has always scared hell out of me."

Ted smiled at him. "I guess it does most people. It did me until I got used to it. You know, I took three months there. When you become a specialist in Anteroom procedures, you must be put in one of the beds and put to sleep for a period of time so you know exactly what it feels like."

"What does it feel like?"

"Like cuddling off to a good, sound sleep in a comfortable bed."

"Do you dream?"

"Yes, sometimes. I dreamed a little bit, pleasant dreams, and then I woke up and it was just like waking up the next morning. I couldn't tell how long I'd been asleep. I was stiff, of course, and it took me a few days to get over the effects of having been in bed for three months, but otherwise it was just like a night's sleep."

"Sometimes, of course," John said, thoughtfully. "But most of the time you don't wake up."

"That's true, but the point is, my old friend, you can. The people in the Anteroom who otherwise would be living lives of exceeding discomfort, in extreme cases torture, are lying peacefully and soundly asleep and sometimes dreaming. But they are alive, they are not dead. They can be waked up, after almost any period of time. If a new and decisive cancer cure should be discovered, we could wake up the patient to whom it could be applied and perhaps cure him. You see? On the other hand, when the time comes that a patient would die, he dies in his sleep. He never knows it; he has no fear concerning it; he has no worries; he has nothing except sleep."

"And you say patients in the Anteroom do dream?"

"Yes, they do. I had some wonderful dreams when I was there."

"But nightmares—what a horrible thing it would be to get involved in a nightmare and be unable to wake up."

"Impossible. As you know, when you're put into the Miller bed, after having been put to sleep, sensors and tubes are attached; your arms and wrists and waist and knees are attached loosely to the bed itself. You are turned several times a day, and exercised, by the bed. You are fed and evacuated automatically. You are warmed, cared for, and your every reaction is registered in your own little computer and controlled there. The equipment is so sensitive that it can tell instantly when the patient begins to dream. It can differentiate between pleasant emotions and unpleasant; pain and fear have a different reaction, and automatically the machine increases sedation when emotion begins to swing from pleasure or serenity into pain and fear. The patient goes deeper to sleep, and the dream stops."

"I guess it's a pretty good thing."

"Well, short of a way of immunizing people against cancer, I think it's the most wonderful invention of the age. It seems to have all the advantages of euthanasia without any of the disadvantages, except for the cost, of course. But then, everybody has health insurance that takes care of the Anteroom. I have a number of complaints against the government, particularly the Norm government, but I must say this aspect of our situation is handled about as well as man can handle it."

"Do some people refuse to be placed in the Anteroom?" John asked.

"There have been a few. We don't try to force it on anyone. It's purely voluntary. Except in the cases of extremely strong-willed individuals, or religious fanatics, they come around after a good deal of needless pain and suffering."

"Religious fanatics?"

"Yes, there still seems to be, in some religions, in some few individuals in those religions, a conviction that a man dying of cancer must suffer terribly intense pain because God intended it to be that way, that for some reason, due to some plan, unknowable by man, God wants that individual to suffer." Ted Carter shook his head. "It seems inconceivable to me, of course, particularly when we know that so much of the cancer is caused now by our own man-made technology, our poisons, our radiation, our food additives, and all the many items that do contribute toward it."

"Well, hell," John said, "you say I've got ten years of activity without pain, and still doing the things I like to do, grouse hunting, skiing even?"

66

"Certainly."

"Fishing?"

Ted laughed, "You go right ahead, John, do all those things you want to do. You're in good health except for this thing, and you'll stay in good health. You come on by every three months or so and let's have a little talk, but other than that there's nothing to do."

"Shall I tell Diana?"

"That's up to you. I wouldn't, if I were you. But that's a decision that you have to make."

"Yes," John said. He shook hands with Ted Carter and went out of his office into the fall day.

It was early September, with only the faintest intimation of the promise of fall in the air. September Song, he thought. A sou'wester was blowing; years ago, when you had a southwest wind, the smog from the overcrowded industrial areas of the country funneled up through Vermont until the mountains looked like dim blurs in the hazy air that prickled lungs and throat. Now there was none of that; even with a sou'wester, the sky was clear except for natural haze. A northeaster could raise true fog, or a fog might blow around from some of the generating-plant cooling towers, but mostly the sky was blue, the weather clear, and the air felt good in your lungs. He knew that the invisible pollution of radiation was in the air, but he couldn't let that bother him. Somehow he felt a vast relief. He had suspected for a long time that he was coming down with *the* thing, cancer, that terrified Roberts. But ten years, good heavens, he could hardly have expected more than ten or fifteen years in any event. He walked the quarter of a mile to his house, up Chipman Hill, down his driveway, through the bushes and trees and past the beautiful sugar maples that he and Diana had planted many years before. They were fine trees now, healthy, smooth-trunked, beautiful in their shapes. There was a touch of gold and red in one of them. At the house he got into old clothes and deliberated between mowing grass and going out and sitting on the carport roof and looking at the view of the Green Mountains four miles to the east. He had just about decided on the carport roof and maybe a cold beer when the phone rang.

"Hello, Martin speaking."

"Hello, Professor Martin?"

"Yes."

"My name is Kirk Patrick. My father wrote—"

"Oh, yes." John remembered the letter that he had received two or three days earlier and, in his distress over his visit to Ted Carter, had nearly forgotten. He didn't exactly feel like talking to some young man now, particularly a young Norm, but he had liked Bob Kirk Patrick; they had been close friends for years, though not closely associated. The times when they had gotten together had been times of warmth and pleasure and good memories.

"How are you, sir?" young Kirk asked. The voice in John Martin's ear seemed to carry a genuine feeling rather than politeness.

"I'm fine, young man," he said. "And you?"

"Oh, I'm swell, of course; how's Mrs. Martin?"

"She seems to be getting younger every day, I must say, and I hope you will write your father to that effect. At the moment she's out at garden club. She should be back in a couple of hours."

"I was wondering, sir, could I possibly come by to see you? My father told me to be sure and do so; and I would want to anyway."

"Why certainly, come ahead." John Martin gave the young man the directions, hung up the phone, and decided he had better have the beer very quickly. He could use it, and it was a little awkward having a drink before a Normal, because of course the Normal, unless he should want to expend a few minutes of his precious budget time, could hardly drink with him. John paused and thought of the wall being raised between the two classes, the Roberts and the Normals, and how even men of good will could never come close together. The suits always separated them, on the Normal or on the Robert. He was on the carport finishing off his can of cold beer when the electric car came soundlessly up the drive. John waved from where he stood, and the figure seen through the transparent oval bubble waved back. John went along the catwalk and stood at the front steps to greet his guest.

"Hello again, Kirk Patrick," he said, holding out his hand; the young man shook hands firmly. John could see through the transparent helmet that he had sandy hair and a bony but attractive face, well freckled, with heavy eyebrows, blue eyes, and a good smile. There hadn't been the slightest touch of hesitation as Kirk put out his hand. Some Normals, even suited, found it difficult to take the hand of a Robert.

"Won't you come in, young man?" John said.

"Yes, sir," Kirk said. "You were sitting on the porch when I drove up. You looked very comfortable to me. Why don't we just sit out there? The sun feels good."

"It does indeed," said John. "I'll let Diana show you the house when she gets back."

"Oh, I probably won't be here that long, sir. I don't want to take up all your time. You must be busy, with school just opening."

"Oh, no," John answered. "I've very little to do during Freshman Week, and my regular schedule leaves me free during much of the daytime, so I can mostly enjoy being out of doors."

"Me, too," Kirk said. "I'm on the night shift down at the plant. I'll do my sleeping in the evening and see the country in my free time."

"Do you like Waybury and Vermont?"

"I sure do, from what I've seen of it so far. I only wish things were the way they used to be, and I could take this suit off and just run in the woods the way you can, sir."

"Well, I understand your feelings, son." John said. "I think you know we have a few disadvantages going with the fact of our freedom here."

"Of course, sir, I'm sorry."

"Come on, let's go sit down."

As they sat on the carport and talked, Kirk mostly about his parents, especially his father, John found his initial feeling of irritation with this young, healthy, Norm powerman evaporating. It was foolish to hold the boy responsible for what society had done. Naturally the suit must be worn. Naturally the two groups had to stay apart. Those people who were clean—how John hated that word—who were Normal, must stay so for the preservation and future of the race. Unless . . . A

70

thought that John had had very often lately tickled the back of his mind, but he put it away for later thinking. It dealt with a young boy of seven named Adam, one of the neighborhood children. Adam had been considered to be a moderately deformed child, and the deformed children were the worst of this whole thing for John. But maybe there was a promise of something more there. He was beginning to suspect it.

Kirk was saying something about the plant, and John brought his attention back to his guest. This young man was well trained, quiet and deferential without being condescending or too deferential. They got into a little argument once about what the power companies had done, and with perfect politeness Kirk held his own quite well. He had been raised in the concept of electrical power and the virtues and need thereof. John liked Kirk, and after a while he offered him a drink. Kirk hesitated.

"No, thank, you, I'll save my budget time for the woods. I do hope, sir, that maybe you'll show me some of the country. I understand you do a lot of hunting, fishing, and walking."

John nodded. "Yes, I get outdoors whenever I can. I'll be very glad to take you, son. Ever do any shooting?"

"Yes, sir. I've done some. I have a shotgun with me."

"Good, we'll certainly plan on getting together. Do you fish?"

"Yes, sir."

"All right, fine, before long we'll take a whack at that. I have a nice place we can go, a little lake to the south of us."

"Someone's coming, sir. It looks like a girl." Another electric car pulled up beside Kirk's. John stretched his neck a little bit.

"Oh, yes, it's my daughter, Anne. She teaches down at the elementary school."

"What does she teach?"

"Oh, a little bit of everything, since she's a second grade teacher. She has the seven-year-old children, and of course at that age you teach mostly self-confidence and thought analysis and—uh—consideration and manners, and a little bit of numbers and how to read. I guess reading is the biggest thing."

"I would think so."

John went to meet Anne at the front steps.

"Hello, Dad," she said. She was a sunny and happy girl. It made John happy just to look at her. That sunny, cheerful, sometimes-squalling baby had suddenly become changed into this beautiful young woman who stood looking quizzically at him.

"What are you staring for, Dad?"

"Oh, hon, it's just once in awhile you look at someone and you really see them." She had golden-brown hair and blue eyes, and a slightly round face through which the cheek bones showed. She was beautiful. Even if she was his daughter, she was beautiful. Her face structure resembled Diana's, that was the reason. She was of medium height and she moved well, like the good athlete she was. She liked doing things, and she loved the children she taught. She was twenty-five and not yet married and there didn't seem to be any strong prospects for the future. John sighed a little at the thought of that. He couldn't blame young people for not wanting to get married and not wanting to have children, with the risks that lay in the process now.

"Who's the Norm on the porch with you, Dad? Someone new at the college?"

"His name is Kirk Patrick. His father was a classmate of mine at the academy, and we have been friends for many years. Kirk is a powerman at the Dunmore plant."

"Oh!"

John could see his own first reactions flash through Anne for a moment as she frowned. The combination of Normal and power was enough to make any Robert feel a little hesitation about friendship.

"He's a nice young man, Anne, very pleasant, just like his father," John said as they went to the porch. "You'll like him. I do, and I was kind of mad when he got here." John enjoyed seeing the effect on Kirk as he introduced Anne. The young fellow kept staring at her. In a few minutes Anne warmed up toward Kirk. There was no doubt this young fellow was likable. He seemed really sincere, not one of the flashy professional envoys of good will attempting to reconcile Roberts to the presence of the atomic power plants over which they had no control. John smiled to himself when Anne offered Kirk a drink.

Kirk said, "Yes, thank you. I can take fifteen minutes of budget time." John caught his eye and winked. Kirk turned a little red and then grinned back.

"What are you two grinning at each other for?"

Anne said. "It must be some joke I don't know about."

"Whatever it is," John said, "there are lots and lots of jokes that you don't know about, young lady. Now you run along and get Kirk's drink. Have one yourself." Anne went inside.

John turned to his guest, "You don't have to worry, Kirk, I keep some clean"—he couldn't help putting the little accent on the word—"water and ice cubes in my house, because Waybury is coeducational, as you know, and sometimes Normal colleagues or students do visit me here."

"Yes sir," said Kirk. He looked his host squarely in the eye, and John Martin could see the regret and pain in his face. "I'm awfully sorry, sir. If there were anything I could do about it, I would."

"Never mind, young man, it is not your fault. Never mind whose fault it is, it's here and with us, and it's up to us to make the best we can of it. I'm glad that you came by."

Kirk reluctantly zipped up his helmet again at the end of fifteen minutes. After that things were a little more constrained then they had been during the quarter hour of true face-to-face, during which John had withdrawn from the conversation, watching with pleasure the enjoyment that these two young people took with one another.

As Kirk drove down the driveway, Anne stood with her hand lightly on the railing, looking after the car and smiling faintly.

"I told you he was a nice fellow," John said.

"You're right, Dad, he didn't seem the way some of the Normals are. Some of them look at me as if I were inferior."

"You find fools everywhere," John said. "This boy certainly doesn't feel that way."

"He doesn't seem to, he's nice."

"Your mother will be home soon. I hope you can stick around for a while."

"Yes, I can, Dad. I wanted to see Mom anyway. What beautiful flowers she has this fall! Excuse me, I'm going to go down and take a closer look."

"Okay." John watched her walk across the lawn over to the farthest flower bed. It was ablaze with gold and white, pink and purple. He stood looking after her, feeling much better now. Meeting young Kirk had brought a satisfaction to his day that he had not felt before.

Chapter Three /

ANNE

John Martin was busy with students and the opening of the college year, and Anne was engaged with a room full of thirty or so young demons who were, she insisted, also young angels. During that first week Kirk spent much of his time wandering in the woods and mountains. Late in the week he went to see Will Aaron, his classmate from Arizona college days and now an assistant professor of economics at Waybury College. He found Will in his office in a normalized building; Kirk was thankful that he could unzip his helmet and relax.

Will was tall and slender; he tended to gesture excessively as he talked, which was about all that Kirk had ever found wrong with him. They chatted for a while in the book-lined office, then went to the faculty lounge to have coffee. Among the dozen or so faculty members there was a good-looking girl who was introduced to Kirk as Joan Pillsbury, a poetry teacher. He met three men, all bearded; Kirk had a poor memory for names, and he classified these three in accordance with beard styles: Goat, Spade, and Mop.

"What do you think of Waybury so far as you have seen it?" asked the latter.

"Oh, come, you shouldn't ask him that!" said a plump, vivacious female who taught philosophy. She tittered and went on. "But of course, I suppose first impressions from an intelligent, educated man may be helpful. How *do* you like Waybury College, Mr. Patrick?"

"Beautiful campus, and your faculty seems very broad, and, oh, intelligent and qualified. I like what I've seen of the students. How does the coeducation work, by the way?"

"Very well," said Goat, stroking his little beard. "A very healthy thing, and the students seem to get along well together. But half of the classes are held in unnormalized rooms, and it does cramp one's style a bit when one has to wear a suit and helmet. It seems to diminish the rapport one hopes to establish with one's students."

Spade took a sip of coffee. "I find it a help in lecture courses. If I think I'm not getting through properly, all I do is turn up my volume. I can awaken even back-row sleepers that way." He tittered.

Mop scratched his head. He has so much hair on his chin, cheeks, head, and eyebrows that Kirk itched when he looked at him. "There certainly is one aspect of the college you probably haven't observed yet. I mean the number of fossils we have around, and I don't mean the interesting exhibits of the geology department." There was general laughter.

"Fossils?" said Kirk, puzzled.

"Yes, certainly, maybe you've met them. People like Martin—Square John, the students call him— who teaches writing. His books aren't worth reading. Just froth. And then there's Gregory Mainyard in the American literature department. He's a very crude fellow, really very crude. Ron Trout, others."

"And don't forget Gene Forrest in our biology department," put in a man who had ordinary hair, features, and eyes, but who worked his mouth around incessantly, as if he were sucking on a particularly repugnant gumdrop. Kirk decided Slurp would be a good name for him. "Gene is so old-fashioned that he doesn't care much for the microscope; he likes to study biology out of doors on field trips. Can you imagine that? And he is very concerned about what's happening to animals and plants in Robert country. But then he's a Robert himself, so one cannot expect too much."

"Why do you call them the fossils?" Kirk asked, feeling a warm surge of anger. He didn't know Mainyard or Gene Forrest or Ron Trout. He did know John Martin, and liked him very much.

"Oh, that's just our little joke," said Mop. "The college has kept them on because, well, it's not easy to get Robert professors who are well qualified. All of these fellows went to excellent schools; of course standards weren't quite as high then in the Ivy League as they are now. But they were very qualified men in their day."

"Yes," said Goat, "but that was a long time ago." And all of them laughed together.

Joan Pillsbury said, "You better be careful talking like this; the president doesn't like it, and Donna says it spoils the whole atmosphere of the college. She says that it smacks of Robertism."

"Who's Donna?" Kirk asked.

"She's the dean of Roberts. Of course, she would feel that way."

"Dean of Roberts?"

"Oh, yes, we have a dean of Roberts; you know, she takes care of the Robert students. A Norm can't really get on a good basis with a Robert. So we must have a dean of Roberts; we have a dean of Norms too, Tom Fetch, who is doing an excellent job."

"Well," said Will Aaron, getting up, "they're not bad. I rather like them, as a matter of fact. Except, of course, for Mainyard. Really, no one could like him. I hate to leave this company, but I have a class coming up in half an hour, and I've got to get ready for it."

Kirk got up too. "I left my suit in your office. I'll come down and pick it up and then run along."

"Oh, no hurry," said Will, "no hurry." They went out into the carpeted corridor and down the stairs, chatting together about old times at the University of Arizona.

"How did you like the Pillsbury?" Will said, as Kirk was putting on the suit.

"Pillsbury? Oh, Joan Pillsbury, the English teacher."

"Yes, the pretty brunette."

"Oh, I thought she was very attractive."

"Oh, she's a nice girl. She dances very well too, if you need a little exercise. Why don't you drop in? Should I give her a call and tell her you'd like to come back?"

The thought interested Kirk, but somehow between the Pillsbury lush figure and bright smile there interposed the grave, sometimes cheerful face of Anne Martin.

"No thanks," he said. "I'm taking it easy for a while."

"Well, I suppose so, up here. You won't have too many opportunities, out among the Roberts as you are, and I don't suppose you have many girls at the power plant. But if you want to drop up here anytime, I think that Miss Pillsbury probably would be interested. Of course there are always women students available, if you don't mind primitive art. By the way, there's a faculty party Saturday night. It's mixed, and it's up at the Snow Cup, the ski area, really a lovely background for a party."

"Indeed!" Kirk said.

"Why don't you come? I'd be delighted to have you as my guest. Bring somebody, if you'd like."

Kirk paused with his helmet half zipped up. "I may bring someone? Could I bring a Robert?"

"Of course; who did you have in mind?"

"I thought I'd ask Anne Martin."

"Anne Martin? She would be most welcome; she really is a delightful girl. I saw you get a little red in the face when they started mentioning John Martin. He's a fine old man, and I think it's a dreadful shame that Anne should be a Robert."

"So do I," said Kirk.

"She's a very sweet person," Will Aaron said. "But won't the party be a little dull for you? You can't touch her unless you're wearing your suit and your gloves. What satisfaction would there be in that?"

Kirk smothered the quick irritation. He hadn't

thought about touching her physically. Maybe he could touch her mind, and that interested him more now then any other contacts. The prospect of being with Anne and really getting to know and to understand her made the idea of any exercise with Joan Pillsbury seem dull.

Kirk walked across the campus, noting that the trees were beginning to show touches of red and gold for fall, and admiring the buildings and the spacing as he went. It was a beautiful campus, built on a ridge; to his right, beyond some dormitories, he could see the Adirondack Mountains beyond the hazy mist that lay always above Lake Champlain. He went into Munroe, one of the old buildings, not normalized, and found John Martin's office. He knocked.

"Come in," John said.

Kirk was received with quiet warmth. The office was long and narrow, with one side covered with books, pictures on the walls, and a picture of Anne and Diana on the desk.

"Sit down, Kirk. Looking over the college?"

"Yes, in a way." Kirk leaned against the table; he felt the impulse of an old childhood gesture, to scratch his head at moments of suspense, to rub his sandy hair which was normally ruffled anyway. He did so. Perfectly possible with these flexible helmets.

"I just want to ask a quick question, sir." Kirk said, "Do you mind if I ask Anne to go to the faculty club Snow Cup party with me?"

Martin took his pipe from his mouth and grinned at Kirk.

"Of course you can ask her, Kirk. Nice of you to

ask me first, but Anne kills her own snakes and makes up her own mind. She likes you, I know, but whether or not she'll want to go to the party with a *Norm*"—John grinned at Kirk—"I don't know."

He had accentuated "Norm" in just the same way that George Sneck had "Robert."

"Thank you," Kirk said. "I hope she does."

"Me, too," John Martin said.

Anne did say yes when he almost timidly asked.

Though Anne had her own small apartment downtown, he was to pick her up at her parents' house. He arrived there at sunset. The Green Mountains were a raspberry-pink in color, and a few clouds above them glowed warmly. The air was still; the birds were singing and there was a crispness in the air. The moon was a silver dollar already beginning to glow in the sky above the mountains. When Kirk came to the door, Mrs. Martin opened it for him.

"Hello, Kirk," she said. "Come in."

"Good evening, Mrs. Martin," Kirk said, coming through the door, wishing he could remove a hat. He made the half-salute that had come to be accepted as a substitute, on the part of a helmeted, suited man, for the gesture of courtesy.

"Anne is with John down in the study. She'll be right up, I'm sure. By the way, if you're going to start dating my daughter you'd better call me Diana, not Mrs. Martin."

"Yes, ma'am."

"Yes, who?"

"Oh. Yes, Diana."

"Good!"

They went into the living room. Its glass walls

faced the Green Mountains. Kirk knew Mrs. Martin must be almost as old as her husband, but as she stood looking out into the mountains, her dark hair carefully coiled around her shapely head, she didn't look very much older than Anne. In this pose her face was sad, her hazel eyes very large. Kirk thought her to be a very handsome person, and he was pleased at her attitude today. Before, she had been a little cool toward him, but of course it was a natural thing for her to feel a considerable reserve in talking to any Norm. They chatted for a few moments and then Anne came in. She was dressed informally in beautifully tailored slacks, walking shoes, blouse, and a sweater. Her hair was in a ponytail. When she came into the room, Kirk felt as if somebody had poured a warm drink down his throat and it had spread all over inside of him. He took both her hands in his gloved ones and she smiled at him and shook her head, waving the ponytail.

"The plastic age," she said. "Isn't it a shame, Mom, to have your boyfriend come all done up in plastic like this?"

Kirk's heart thumped. "You say the word, Anne," he said, grinning, "and I'll pull the zipper and get out of the plastic." He was joking, of course, and both the ladies laughed. But Kirk found himself giving an involuntary glance at the left hand of each, where the orange R stood strong and evil, and both women saw it. He didn't know what to do to make up for the blunder, but then he looked at Anne again and saw that it was not necessary for him to do anything at all. She understood. He felt that she always would understand everything he would ever do, and that always there would be warmth and tolerance for him behind those blue eyes.

Kirk had not yet been to the Snow Cup, and as they drove through the evening afterglow he found the trip delightful. The road wound up a mountain, wall to the right and sheer drop into a canyon to the left. It descended again, met the river, smashing and gurgling its way down the mountain, low now with the dryness of September. Then the way led across another bridge, then up onto a plateau with other peaks rising above it on all sides, tips pink-tinged with the last of the light. Anne sat beside him, smiling, talking a little, pointing out the Dragon's Den, the Robert Frost memorial, and the Waybury College summer campus. An endless carpet of forest swept up from the edge of Bread Loaf campus, ending at last in the high, square shape of Bread Loaf Mountain. The road climbed some more through spruce woods, then turned right into the Snow Cup, a circular valley surrounded by mountains on all sides. The glass-walled lodge faced the closest mountains, upon which were two ski jumps, a double chair lift, and the wide swathes of trails coming down through the woods. Beyond the lodge and connected to it was a second lodge building, also facing the jumps.

"That's the normalized annex," Anne said. "You can eat and drink in there. I won't be able to go there with you, because I didn't bother to bring my suit."

"If you can't go there, damned if I will!" Kirk exclaimed.

"Oh, sure. You have to have a drink and some

dinner. Don't worry; I won't feel insulted. I'm going to have a drink, I do hereby heartily assure you."

"I've saved some budget time," Kirk said. "We can have at least one drink together."

"Fifteen minutes." Her voice was sad. "Isn't it a shame for two people to have only an hour a week when that plastic wall isn't between them?"

"Yes." He felt as if he wanted to cry. "It's a shame."

A fire burned in the big fireplace. The tables had been pulled near the windows. Night was falling outside and moonlight was growing stronger. The firelight flickered. People were singing songs, many sitting on the floor or on the raised platform before the hearth. The unsuited Roberts held glasses; the suited Norms were smiling. Everyone seemed affable and happy.

"I'm going to take my budget time for the first drink, Anne," Kirk said. "Will you have one?"

"Yes, certainly. We'll go out on the terrace and watch the mountains and the moonlight."

Kirk asked for two Canadian whiskies with water, and they went outside. Other couples were on the terrace, still others strolling. The sound of a nearby brook was pleasant in the night. From inside came the sound of voices, laughter, and music. The mountain rose above them silent and majestic in the moonlight. The moon was so bright that Kirk could detect a dark blueness in the sky itself, and only the brightest stars were visible. The tower of the largest ski jump loomed angularly against the bright sky.

"I'm looking forward to the jumping at Carnival," Kirk said. "I've never seen a live ski jump."

"We've got some good jumpers," Anne said. "Of course its hard for a Robert to be successful in international skiing, because it's very difficult for him to travel."

"I understand. Let's not think about it."

They pledged each other and then didn't talk much anymore as they sat close together on a bench. Kirk had his helmet unzipped. The minute minder on his wrist watch was ticking away, marking the seconds until his budget time expired.

"Anne, I want you to know how much it means to have you with me tonight."

"Thank you. It meant something when you asked me, too. Isn't it silly? Isn't it crazy?"

"Yes. I guess it is. But it's a wonderful thing all the same."

"How long will you be in Waybury, Kirk?"

"I'll be here for a year. Maybe then I can extend for another." He knew that an extension would be highly unlikely. The company didn't encourage its powermen to become attached to any one area. It was customary to alternate Robert-country and Norm-country tours to keep the powermen clean. The use of that word, clean, even silently in his own thoughts, irritated Kirk, because by its implications Anne was not clean. She was dirty. The orange R glowed in the dark on her left hand. They finished the drinks and Kirk zipped up his helmet with the ding of the minute minder. Anne smiled at him, but there were tears in her eyes, and he felt his own eyes wet with an irrational, unreasonable sadness. He took both her hands.

"Oh, Anne!" She didn't answer, but he felt the response of her hands on his, even through the gloves.

Later, while Anne settled down to a plate of beef stew and a glass of wine, Kirk went through the air lock into the normalized half of the lodge. It was newer and more luxurious, but without a fireplace. Most of the Norms were there, helmets removed; some of them had removed their suits as well, indicating that they were here for the evening. Kirk saw the Goat talking to Mop and Spade, and Joan Pillsbury, her suit off, her breasts showing firm and round through the transparent panel of her cocktail dress. Kirk didn't like gold nipplestick. She was talking animatedly to two young faculty members, both unsuited. She waved at him as he entered. As he picked up his drink, Kirk heard Mop talking to Spade and Goat.

"Isn't this a bore? I hate this party, like all the faculty club parties. It's having all the Roberts, of course. One feels sorry for them, but one simply does not want to be with them socially, and I feel the strain. One can't be one's proper self."

"I agree, utterly," Spade said. "I wish Prexie didn't insist on it, but he does feel that the faculty should get together at regular intervals. After all, we have common goals, the good of the students, the college, the country—not to mention the cultivation of some good minds that can properly assess art, life, and literature. We must have culture. Even the Roberts must have culture."

Kirk thought of Anne outside in the other room with the orange R glowing on her hand. He downed the drink with savage haste, picked up a couple of sandwiches, ate them quickly, had a cup of coffee and another drink, and went back to Anne.

They walked up one of the trails to a small lake that shone in the moonlight like quicksilver. It was probably as clean as a lake could be in Robert country. It lay high in the mountains, deep, clear, surrounded by peaks with only the towers of the chair-lift to remind Kirk of man's mechanical invasions of nature. It was too small to be a nuke cooling pond, and the nearest air plant was a good distance away; its noise was only a sigh in the distance. Kirk and the girl didn't speak much at the lake. They just sat together in wordless content. He was sorry that he had used up his budget time, but it really didn't matter. He thought how lovely it would be to take Anne in his arms, and he had the feeling that had he been a young Robert she would not have objected. But as it was, no. The training was too closely ingrained in him. One couldn't touch a Robert. The reason was a purely physical, medical reason, he knew that. Contact was dangerous, that was why Roberts were always suited in Normal country. But he could see that on the part of some people, quite intelligent people like Mop and Spade, this physical barrier was rapidly growing into an intellectual and social barrier. Mop had actually been speaking of the Roberts as if they were inferior, not simply unfortunate people who had been gradually and increasingly exposed for years to radiation that some segments of technology had insisted, to the end, did not exist. Power plants had been thought to be perfectly safe. Kirk looked at Anne and put his suited arm around her shoulder. She looked up to him and smiled, and again he saw the moonlight sparkle in the tears in her eyes.

When he took her home after the party, neither of them were saying very much. She didn't invite him in.

"It's been a wonderful evening, Anne," he said. "I've enjoyed it."

"Thank you, Kirk. I've enjoyed it too, and you know this is the first date I've had with a Norm."

"I certainly hope that it won't be the last," he said. "I've enjoyed it. Good night, dear."

"Good night, Kirk." The door closed.

Kirk broke the speed limits getting back to the plant. He was safe, he knew, since Frank Owen had agreed to extend his own shift to whatever time was necessary, and the substitution had been approved by the supervisor. It was quite usual for the technicians to take shifts or parts of shifts for one another. He got back early enough so that he only owed Frank one hour, by the time he went in to the main board with everything else driven from his mind but the job before him. Even through the inflexible discipline of the watch, the vision of Anne, warm, alive, gently smiling, but with tears in her eyes, kept intruding between himself and the dials of the board.

The next morning he visited Anne in her class-room at the Waybury Elementary School.

Chapter Four /

THE BIRDS AND THE BEES

Kirk had been in Waybury for three weeks and was feeling thoroughly at home when George Sneck called him into his office. He nodded at Kirk and continued a phone conversation. Kirk sat down at ease, for George Sneck was not a powermaster, only a powerchief. He looked at the usual picture of Meredith above Sneck's desk. On the other wall hung the VPC map of Vermont. He went over to study it a little more closely. Scattered fairly evenly along the map by rivers or lakes of varying sizes were thirty white lights. Kirk easily picked out this plant on Dunmore, the one halfway between Rutland and Waybury on Otter Creek, and the one just above Vergennes on Otter Creek. A long string of plants lay along Lake Champlain. Another long string glowed on the other side of Vermont, on the Connecticut River. A cluster of lights glowed in the Northeast, cooled by the large lakes found in the Northeast Kingdom. Five red dots scattered on the map indicated the positions of plants being built. Three blue lights indicated the sites for planned plants. Kirk really didn't see where the number of plants in Vermont was to be very greatly increased. On the lower stretches of

Otter Creek and on the Connecticut River and even northern Lake Champlain it was becoming increasingly difficult to get sufficient cooling, for the water was pretty warm. Sportsmen, fishermen, closet conservationists, and others were extremely unhappy about the heat in all the major streams and bodies of water in Vermont, but Kirk only shrugged at the thought. Too bad, but mankind must have power, and the demand for it constantly increased. True, population was pretty well stabilized now, but the power supply would be a long time catching up with the demand. Also, the more plants there were, the more radiation there was; consequently more air plants, more water deradiation plants and deradders were necessary. The increased power they required then increased radiation again. Kirk sighed. The prospect didn't look too good. Power companies were satisfied with the plants they now possessed. The Atomic Energy Commission and the Nuclear Regulatory Commission, which had become all-powerful in anything pertaining to atomic energy, were still saying that the newest plants were clean and safe, even though any powerman knew that they produced radiation. The AEC insisted that the radiation in Robert country was caused by older plants, built before proper technology had been developed. Sneck came up behind Kirk, breaking his thoughts.

"Think there's room for a few more there, hey, Kirk? Well, maybe you'll have one of them someday. Well, son, I just called you in to see how you're getting along. Your work is okay, but sometimes Robert country is hard to adjust to. Any problems?"

"Why, no, sir," said Kirk, "I'm getting along pretty well. I like Robert country."

"Yeah, I hear you're seeing quite a bit of some Roberts up in town. Is that right?"

"Yes, sir, they're nice people. I like them very much."

"Well, don't overdo it, son, don't overdo it. That's all, Kirk."

Relieved, Kirk left the room. He had feared that some extra duty awaited him that would have kept him at the plant all day. Now he could accept John Martin's invitation to drop by and have a drink and meet a few friends. Not a cocktail party, just some people coming by.

When Kirk arrived at the Martins', he saw Diana with several women down on the lower lawn, looking over the flower beds. She waved a greeting and pointed up at the carport roof. John was standing there beckoning him up. Anne was not with Diana, so Kirk went up the steps and out onto the porch. Four or five men were seated there talking among themselves, each with a drink in his hand. A magnificent golden Labrador with the white hairs of age in his muzzle was lying very quietly behind one of the chairs, his amber eyes unblinkingly fastened on the large man who sat in it.

"Glad you could come over, Kirk," John said. "Anne is not here yet. How about a drink?"

"No thank you, John," Kirk said, "I think I'll save my budget time until Anne gets here."

"Aha!"

Kirk found himself blushing. "That's right, sir."

"Okay, come along and I'll introduce you."

There was a very special warmth in John's voice

as he introduced Kirk to these men. Kirk knew they were people of whom his host thought a great deal, so he tried with a special emphasis to remember the names and to hook them to the people who bore them. First was Gregory Mainyard, and Kirk was sure he would always remember him because of one feature. He concentrated so hard on it that he almost missed the next names—Joe Ball, Gene Forrest, Jim Mann, and Charley Morgan. Kirk was sensitive enough to notice the restraint and the slight awkwardness in the group. It could not be otherwise, he knew, since he was a Normal and a powerman. Only John and Charles Morgan seemed perfectly at ease. They all shook hands with him; again there was the unpleasant fact of his gloved hand, and on their left hands the fluorescent Rs of vivid orange.

Gregory Mainyard was a spirited, broad-shouldered man. His face was lined and stern with a rather shaggy moustache, and he had thick, curling gray-red hair, bushy eyebrows, very sharp light blue eyes, and not a trace of a smile about him. The hand that he reached toward Kirk was broad and muscular and callused; on each temple, almost hidden in the thick, short hair, grew a small, curved, sharp-pointed horn about an inch and a half long. "Hullo," he grunted.

Charles Morgan looked to be made of weathered leather and steel. The bones of his face showed through and his eyes were very clear and interested. He had the wrinkles of smiles on his face in mouth corners and eye corners, and he spoke warmly and well to Kirk as they met.

The other two men were talking about ducks.

"Hey, Joe, Jim. Let me make you known to Kirk Patrick here, son of an old friend," John said.

Joe Ball, short and square, barely moved as he stood up, reached out a hand, and with a very good smile said, "Hi."

When Jim Mann stood up, the golden Lab lifted his head and looked at him intently. Jim reached out a long arm and a big hand and said, "Pleased to meet you, Mr. Patrick." His face was tanned, his hair short-clipped. He had very broad shoulders and was by far the largest man there.

Even through the constraint, Kirk could feel warmth and friendliness in this group. He was about to sit down when he noticed a group of children running across the drive. They paused a little bit below and to one side of the porch. Two or three little girls and several boys stood discussing something earnestly. Kirk recognized one of the boys.

"It's Adam," he said. "Adam Dabney, isn't it?"

"Yes," said John Martin. "Have you met Adam?"

"Yes, sir, I visited Anne's school the other day. I was very much impressed. Will you excuse me a moment? I'd like to go down and say hello to him."

"Sure, go ahead."

Kirk ran down the steps, walked across the yard, and saw Adam's large head and then his face looking at him with the clear, bright smile that had so attracted him in the school room. Immediately the feeling of uneasiness at the size of the head vanished. Actually, it was not as large as that of an adult. It was simply large to be the head of a seven-year-old boy; if it continued to grow it would always look a little large, though not freakish. Just a big head.

"Hi," Adam said casually.

"Good afternooon, Adam," Kirk said.

Adam smiled again at him and nodded his head; he looked down at the ground and scuffed his shoes.

"I'm glad to see you again, Adam," Kirk said.

Again the smile, large blue eyes, and the voice that said clearly and quietly, "Thank you."

The other children were dashing away. Adam looked at them and then back to Kirk, evidently torn between loyalty to his playmates and a feeling of necessary politeness to this giant adult encased in the transparent suit.

Kirk said, "So long, Adam. Good-bye."

Adam ran away with the other children.

On the carport above, John said to his friends, "See, I told you, that's the kind of fellow he is. You know that some of the people we've had here think of a Robert as inferior. This young fellow seems to like us, and he's got brains too. And Anne likes him."

"He's still a goddamn Normal," growled Gregory.

"I like him," Charley said. "I think he's got sense."

"Maybe we *could* use him," Gregory said.

Joe Ball nodded his head, and nodded again looking at John. Just then, Kirk came back up onto the porch.

"What can you do with that poor little bastard?" Gregory asked Kirk when he returned. "Too bad to see a kid retarded like that. Hell, that's the oldest one around, and he can't even talk very well yet."

"Maybe," Kirk said, remembering Anne.

"I'm not so sure," John Martin put in. "I saw him do a nice thing last summer. A baby robin had gotten out of the nest; he could fly a little bit, he'd taken off on his first flight, but I guess he had overestimated his capability, because he got caught in the wind and was stuck out there in the middle of the lawn, flopping around a little. He would have gotten up eventually, but some of the little bastards that live on the other side of the road came by and started pegging rocks at him. One of them hit him and hurt him some, and I was on my way there to kick their asses off the place when Adam came running up like a fury. You know how quiet and pleasant and sweet he is? He wasn't sweet that day; he was kicking them, hitting them and flying at them like a doggone wildcat. They were getting ready to slap him around a little when I got there and packed them off. Adam went over and picked up that hurt bird, and he wasn't happy until we put him in a large shoe box with a little pan of water in there for him to drink and Kleenex for him to flop on, and stuck him up in the limbs of that cedar tree over there, in the sun, where a cat wouldn't be likely to get him. He was gone the next day and I didn't see any feathers, so I think he was just dazed and got over it, and his ma located him and he made out all right. But it's the first time I have ever seen one of these big-headed children turn violent, and it was the boys hurting that bird that really set him off."

"I like that little guy," Kirk said. "And I don't think he's retarded either, Mr. Mainyard."

Gregory grunted, "You like him, huh! Okay, call

me Gregory; I'm not used to all this mister stuff. John here says that you want to go on a grouse hunt when the season is open. You like gunning?"

"I certainly do," Kirk said. "I haven't had a chance to do much recently, but I brought my 20-gauge with me. I used to love to hunt out in the southwest, but there aren't many places left now."

"No, I guess not in Normal country. They're pretty well growing food on all the land there, aren't they?"

"Just about."

Gregory grunted and nodded. Kirk was unable to refrain from looking again at the short white-colored horns almost hidden in the thick hair at his temples. John Martin saw his glance. "Those things bother you any, Greg?" he asked.

"Oh, hell, not much. A little ache there now and then, but I kind of like them." Gregory laughed. "You know, the other day one of them Ellises was giving me some heat down at the store because I shot a tire off his car when he was jacking deer in my driveway. He said that if I wasn't so old he'd have beat hell out of me, and that he was goin' to do any huntin' he wanted to around here anytime, and if he wanted to jack a deer it was his own business, by Jesus! Well, I didn't say a thing. I just lowered my head and butted him in the stomach."

A roar of laughter spread over the group.

"That's our Greg," somebody said.

"What happened?" John asked, grinning.

"He got the hell out of there," Gregory said. "Christ, I never saw anybody run so goddamn fast. I'm kind of sorry I did it now. I could have broke his arm in a minute if he'd have tried anything."

"You see, Kirk," John said, "Greg, here, is a kind of stubborn; he won't have his fruit or game deradded. Anything else, but not fruit or game. The doctors told him it might bring about some special changes in his body."

"Screw 'em," growled Mainyard. "They can plant me when they want to, but until they do, screw 'em. Venison tastes like crap after it's spent a day in one of those redadders."

"Do you take the shots?" Kirk asked.

"Yep, I got a few people I want to scrag before I go."

Everybody smiled. Kirk thought there was a particular look in some of the smiles exchanged, particularly that of Charley Morgan. John laughed.

"Greg also wants to stick around until he's bred a dog that can talk. He's getting pretty close to it with Bumps, now, aren't you, Greg?"

"Ahh!" Mainyard grunted. "That dog's already got more sense than most of the people sitting here on this porch."

Kirk found himself liking this group of people very much, but he decided that Gregory interested him more than most. He didn't smile much, but when you looked at him you saw that there was a twinkle in his deepset eyes. He had a short curved pipe that he smoked continuously, puffing away, occasionally breaking out into a fluid, vivid exposition of fact or opinion, and once a brief story that held the entire group silent. He was a born raconteur. Gradually most of the attention turned to Charley Morgan, who was talking about bees.

John had mentioned in his introduction that Charley was a bee man. And the subject, the effect that radiation had had on bees, was particularly interesting to Kirk. It appeared that Charley now had two types of bee colonies. One type, much like the old bee except that the individual had increased three times in size, operated just as bees always had. There had been a period of disorganization within the hives, but then they had appeared to become accustomed to the radiation. Charley distributed his hives about the country, where they pollinated crops and fruits and flowers. His other types of swarms were specialized; the bees were the same size as before, but they had lost their wings and their power to fly. Charley had them housed in small, light plastic hives that could be hung from a tree limb. When a fruit man wanted an orchard polinated, Charley would drive out with thirty or forty of these hives. One would be hung in each tree, and the bees walked to the individual blossoms, pollinated them, and returned to the hive with the nectar. There were a lot of bees in these little hives and they worked pretty quickly, taking three or four hours to the tree. They had it pretty well timed; a man walking by could see when activity had ceased and would unhook the hive and take it to another tree. Kirk listened, fascinated and yet sad. It seemed a terrible thing that the bees had been deprived of their power of flight. He was glad that most of Charley's colonies were of the ordinary bee type, merely increased in size.

"How about ants?" Kirk asked.

"Those buzzards are pretty tough. Radiation doesn't seem to hurt them, but they sure know about it. If you place a source of radiation anywhere near an anthill, they'll leave. It hasn't seemed to affect them too much. A little change in size, maybe, and I've seen some pretty big anthills here and there." Charley folded his hands together and looked at his scarred, callused thumbs. "Insects resist radiation pretty well. Size and social organizations are the most affected. I saw a praying mantis the other day that was a foot long. Man, if one that size hooks your finger, you're going to know it!"

"Does it seem to affect birds very much?"

"They've done pretty well. They'll have at least one generation, sometimes two or three, in a year, and they've had time to mutate protectively, since the radiation increase was fairly gradual. Most of the species have survived. Some individual birds have changed in size, depending on the intensity of radiation in their breeding and resting areas. Now and then I see a chickadee the size of a robin, or a robin the size of a crow. But so far they are the exception."

"How about the larger animals, the mammals?"

"Oh, some of them have changed a little," Gregory said, grinning behind his pipe. It was out, so he took a kitchen match from his pocket and struck it on one of his horns. Kirk watched, fascinated. Then Anne arrived and he forgot about the rest of them. At her suggestion, they went for a walk.

As Kirk and Anne walked down the drive, the men on the carport porch watched them go. John could see that the women had gone into the house; from the sounds coming through the screen door, Diana had asked their friends to stay over for grilled hamburgers and corn and tomatoes from the garden. He had expected it, approved, and had plenty of cold beer ready.

"That's a nice young man," Charley Morgan said, looking after them.

"For a goddamn Norm," Gregory Mainyard growled.

"I like him," John Martin said. "I don't know whether he would help us or not, but I've never seen one of their powermen here who had the same attitude toward us that he has. Most of them are totally wrapped up in that nuclear plant, and they get mad if you say something about nuclear power having ruined the world. But this young man seems to sort of agree that they have."

"Maybe he's all right," Gregory said. "But we better know him a good deal longer before we say anything."

"I heartily agree. Charley?"

"Let's keep it quiet."

There was silence on the porch. John thought of this thing they had just been discussing, a matter that had at first been just talk. In the last year it had grown to something more than that. An organization, disguised as the Interstate Hunting and Fishing Association, now was spread all through Vermont and into Maine and New Hampshire. This organization was dedicated to basic changes in the Robert-Norm society and its technology. Not revolution. but reform.

The grievances were all linked. The Roberts had no control of the power plants built in their country. Most of the power was exported to the population centers in Norm country. The profit and the power went to the directors. officers, executives, and stockholders down in Norm country, in the large cities. More plants were being planned and built in Robert country, and the Roberts had no control over sites, size, and whether a plant should be built at all or not. Gradually the Atomic Energy Commission had increased its power to a point where only it could choose a plant site. Once the site was chosen, the AEC had the right of eminent domain, and could take the land and turn it over to the power company making the investment.

Many Roberts realized—and John was sure that Norms did too—that the country was in a deadly, vicious spiral. The power demand increased constantly, for manufacturing, heating, air conditioning, lights, TV, transportation, and a thousand gadgets. It was also used in vast quantities by the air plants that helped clean the air, and by the water deradiation stations that cleaned water sufficiently so that it could be used for irrigation in the dry Normal farm country. The hundreds of thousands of deradders in use drew large quantities of power. More plants were built to supply the power; the plants polluted more, so more power was needed to clean air, water, and food. That power required more plants—John ended the thought on utter discouragement. That was the spiral that must be broken. But how? If Roberts protested about power demands, they were told that the production of the shots that prevented the radiated Roberts from dying of radiation sickness required vast amounts of power. They wouldn't want that cut down, would they?

These shots were manufactured in Normal country; they would keep potency only a short while, so there was never in Robert country enough of the vaccine for more than a couple of months, at most. If this supply should be stopped, then all the Roberts would die.

"Why in the world did the power companies kill solar energy?" John asked in a kind of dumb despair. "It could so easily have been the answer to so many problems."

"Don't be stupid, John," Gregory growled. "You know goddamn well why. Solar power could give every man his own energy source—up here maybe not for all his energy needs, but for a big chunk of them—and the goddamn power companies were scared that people would get away from them. If a man could heat and light his house from his own solar cells—which is perfectly possible, as we all know—he wouldn't give a damn for the power companies. He wouldn't pay them, he couldn't be scared of them. Do you realize that the power companies run this country today? Of course you do. Supermen—the sons of bitches. Well, they would lose all that if they allowed the development of solar power. Of course it would save us all, save them too, but they're so damn greedy they won't see it. It would mean losing part of their market, and part of their power."

Gene Forrest exclaimed in apparent despair. "God, you know, John, back in the twentieth century, when people with sense were trying to have solar power developed instead of nuclear, when the world was still clean, how the goddamn power companies tried to laugh solar power out of existence. Succeeded, too. You just mention solar power to a Normal and he'll laugh his fool head off. Conditioning. Hypnotic, subliminal, speakers under pillows as they sleep, all that sort of thing. Solar energy—haw haw haw. Big joke."

"And the way they train them at the Power Academy," Greg said, shaking his head. "Superconditioning. If a graduate hears the phrase solar energy, or solar power, he laughs like hell. Can't help it. Mention it to young Patrick, John. Ask Anne to mention it to him. He'll laugh. Automatically. Frightening."

"They're stupid," said John. "Why can't they see? A hundred square miles—that's an area ten miles square—out in Arizona or the California desert would furnish enough power for all of New England. There's no problem about long-range transmission any more. Why won't they do it? They'd still control it, and could rob us blind, the way they've always done."

"Just what I said," Gregory grunted. "They're scared to death of solar power. Afraid it would end their domination of the world. And it would, too." He suddenly became furious. "Let's get this thing moving! We should have one foremost demand, by God! No more nuclear plants. Ration electricity, by God, if necessary! Give the goddamn AEC and the NRC not more than three years to develop solar power. Put every penny into it; get the whole government behind it! Can't they see what they are doing?"

"I guess not," John said, his mind busy with the inner vision of a world where again mankind had a future, where the radiated areas might gradually be cleaned up. A world in which his grandchildren might not have to have the orange R on their hands.

The orange R. Somehow it bothered him more than almost anything else. Originally a medical matter, one designed to facilitate detection and treatment of radiation sickness, it had become a social barrier, a class distinction. It had created a class of second-class citizens, the Roberts. They were poorly represented in Congress, because their numbers now were so much less than those of Norm country. They had no Roberts on the Supreme Court, none on the AEC, none on the higher federal benches. Few Roberts could attend the great universities and technical schools in the nation, because the institutions could not accommodate Roberts, had not built sealed dormitories, laboratories, and classrooms. Roberts couldn't travel in Norm country or abroad without permits, and then usually they had to go in groups.

"And another thing," Gregory said, lighting his pipe. "We ought to get royalties on every kilowatt of power produced in Robert country and exported to the Norms. Hell, that would make the states rich enough to really take care of their people. We could built technical schools, universities, if we had to. Take care of the poor. Have good schools."

"You're right," John agreed. "We all know that."

He was convinced that no Roberts wanted to really destroy the system, to upset things. They didn't want to condemn a couple of hundred million people to death. But they wanted to control the power, or have royalties on it, in a decent commercial transaction. They wanted to use the credits so gained for travel, for all the manufactured articles they might have need for or desire for, in short, to have the opportunity that their sacrifice had earned for them. For many years every nuclear plant built had been placed in Robert country, ever since, in fact, the dreadful month in which three plants had ruptured cooling systems, spreading radioactive vapor over much of Vermont, New Hampshire, and western Massachusetts. After that month, no more plants had been built near populated areas; before long, the requirement that the plants should be located on running fresh water and in lightly populated country had brought about the present situation. Norm country was surviving and living high on the power generated in Robert country, where radiation grew worse, year by year.

It was time for a change, John thought. He was not a man of violence, but he was ready to invoke it to bring the change. He and his friends intended to cut the power lines from Plant V7; they intended to take over the plant, if possible. They wanted the movement to spread to plants all over Robert country.

The primary demand would be the development of solar power, followed by the abandonment of the entire nuclear power system, as soon as practicable. Radiation would stop increasing; there would be no more radioactive waste. such as was produced by the fission plants in millions of gallons a year. That cancer of the earth, the area in which these unutterably deadly materials were stored and which had been transformed into a malignant desert—that cancer need not increase. It could not shrink for a thousand years, but they would not have to add to it.

Another thing must be changed. One man, one vote. That theoretically noble idea had brought about much of the sickness of the earth, had created the tyranny of the majority. The great cities, with their tens of millions, ruled everything. The fact that a nuclear plant, placed well away in a sparsely populated area, would poison, sicken, eventually kill the residents of that area, meant absolutely nothing if it meant also that the residents of the city could continue to lavish energy on creature comfort, on luxury, to waste it, throw it away. John was convinced that one man and his well-being *should* be as important to the country as that of ten million men and women in New York. Equal protection of the law. Not: "There are more of us, so we can do anything we want to you and to your country." It was a puzzle, a problem, but one man, one vote—it had to go.

Charley Morgan, the quiet, laughing man over there, had made revolt possible. He had learned how to extract bee venom, in quantities, from his hives of the new, larger bees. Not only did the shots of this venom work against radiation, they were more effective than those furnished by the government. John, with the other men on this porch and five hundred more scattered throughout the northeast, had been taking only Charley's bee venom for the past year. All felt fine—as far as radiation went. John remembered his cancer and grimaced. But that had no connection with the bee-venom shots.

Now there was available a supply of bee venom

sufficient to last the Roberts of Vermont, New Hampshire, and Maine for at least six months.

So now, action was possible.

John hoped the change would be bloodless, without violence. But if it required violence and killing, he was ready. It would come soon, he knew. Certainly within the year. He would die for it if necessary—and that would be a minor sacrifice. But he would do all he could to bring it about. He lifted his glass.

"Okay, boys," he said, grimly. "Here's to the Interstate Hunting and Fishing Association. The sooner the better!"

"Somebody's been feeding you raw meat," Gregory said, with a warm grin around his pipe. "Here's to it, boys!"

Kirk and Anne were walking over a hill a few hundred yards away. The road led to the top of the hill through a town park which was untouched forest, now beginning to show the vivid colors of fall in this fourth week of September. They were talking about the children in Anne's classroom.

Kirk said, "Anne, I never had anything affect me so much. It just made me feel horrible to see those children."

"I used to feel the same way," Anne said. "Though I knew it wasn't my fault. The more I see of them, not the true deforms, for they are a tragedy beyond mention, but these children who aren't so badly handicapped, the better I feel. What did you think of William, the little one-legged man? Did you see him out there? He can handle himself among the children and they don't think it at all strange that he has but one leg. You watch, he'll be an athlete."

"Poor little Adam," Kirk said. "I felt that he wanted to talk so badly, to say more things than he could say, and somehow when I looked at him I wanted to talk to him. Wanted to hear him. I think it is too bad that he should be—well, I was telling your father's friends that I didn't think he was retarded; but it seems a shame that his head should have to be enlarged as it is. It makes an outcast of him."

Anne was quiet as they walked on. Jays called from the woods, a crow cawed above. A couple of chickadees went flirting along in the bushes beside them.

"When I'm around Adam," Anne said, "I can sense something coming from him, a potential that frightens me. I think that when he and the others like him grow up, they might change the world."

Kirk looked at her. He thought of all the things he had seen and learned, of all the years behind him, and of the civilization, which without being willing to admit it was dying, would die someday.

Anne met his eyes.

"It sure could use some changing," Kirk said.

Anne stopped and they looked at each other for a long moment. "I'm so glad you feel that way, Kirk," she said, "so very glad."

Chapter Five /

GROUSE HUNT

September passed gently away and it was October. Haze deepened on the hills; the sun continued to shine while the farmers grumbled about the lack of rain. To Kirk, even enclosed in his suit, life was wonderful. His happiness was, he realized, focused and increased through his almost daily contacts with Anne. Her father and his friends also enriched Kirk's days. He once found himself noticing the orange R on a Robert's hand and thinking that it looked rather nice and that his own hand seemed blank and colorless. He caught himself with a start, then whistled. He must be particularly careful, or the old subconscious might have him making re-peated mistakes that could bring out the glowing orange letter on his own hand. He liked the Roberts, and he strongly suspected he loved one Robert. Certainly Anne did something to his blood-stream and inner mechanism that nothing else had ever been able to do. Still, he didn't want to be a Robert. His situation would be worse than theirs because his transition would be more abrupt—his danger from cancer would be much greater. Kirk's thoughts came back from those matters that had darkened the October day, and he looked with seeing eyes again at the mountain rising above the lake. Only the power lines marred the scene of beauty before him. He had seen Anne last night again, and today, in just about an hour, he would be leaving for Waybury. John Martin had invited him along on a grouse hunt with Gregory and Joe Ball. Kirk had accepted with pleasure; Anne wouldn't be going on the hunt, but he almost certainly would see her afterwards. He hugged that thought to him on the way to Waybury.

John insisted that they use his Beetlelectric. He talked a good deal as they drove down Route 7, through East Waybury, across the bridge over the long pool with the waterfall at the head of it, and wound up the mountain and along by the gorges. Kirk didn't talk much; he was remembering this drive up to the Snow Cup with Anne.

In Ripton they turned off of the main road onto a starkly climbing one and, after mounting a hill, made another right turn onto a dirt road. They were in the mountains now, and it was a scarlet fall, with plenty of gold and bronze, with the evergreens accentuating the brighter colors, all making sharp contrast with the blue sky above. They turned off onto a deeply winding driveway and passed a neat barn and a fenced field where a dozen sheep grazed. Beyond the barn was a pasture, and Kirk saw several cows and a couple of horses grazing in comfortable coexistence. The grass was beginning to turn brown from the first frost. The house was a colonial to which structures had been added, and its outer covering of shingles was silvered to a weathered gray. A four-wheel drive, heavy-duty electric with a snowplow was parked in the back, with another lighter-duty four-wheel drive.

"I see Joe is already here," John said. "Oh, here comes somebody." A grayish blue long-haired dog came trotting quite casually around the corner of the house, stopped for a moment, looked them over, gave one sharp bark, and trotted forward to John.

"Hello, Bumps," said John. He held out a hand, Bumps sniffed it. "Bumps, this is Kirk Patrick." Bumps looked intently into Kirk's face, sat down, barked once and held up a paw.

Kirk took the paw and shook it and said, "Pleased to meet you, Bumps. Is it sir or ma'am?"

"Ma'am," John said. "This is Bumps the umpteenth. Pointing griffon. Greg swears by 'em."

"Hi, boys," Joe Ball said from the breezeway. "I think that dog's got more sense than Greg has."

"Right," said John. "It just can't tell stories quite as well."

"Liz says come on in," Joe said. "Greg is down in the basement thrashing around at something. I think he's rousting season-before-last's grouse out of the freezer to make room for the ones he's going to get today."

Elizabeth Mainyard was a tall woman with bright red hair and a face that showed breeding, personality, toughness, and undying good humor. Kirk had met her briefly at John's house. There were no formalities now, other than: "I'm pleased to see you, Kirk. Glad you could make it."

"Are you coming with us?" Kirk asked.

"Nope, not today. I've got some housecleaning to

do. Besides, there are four of you, and that's really enough in the woods with the dog."

"I'll only be a spectator," Kirk laughed,

"Why? Aren't you shooting?"

"Well, yes, I've got a gun along, but I'm not exactly the fastest gun in the West."

Liz smiled. "You'll find yourself getting first shots," she said. "Greg and these other bums talk kinda tough, but they're really very generous when they're out hunting."

Gregory came up from the cellar shortly thereafter and was attacked by Joe and John for lateness, keeping the freezer full of birds, distilling rum in the basement, and a dozen other shady activities. Joe said that Bumps had probably told Greg to go down in the cellar and stay a while because he had misbehaved that morning. Greg snorted, "For Christ sake, are we going huntin' or are we not? Let's get moving."

"We're waiting for you, Gregory," John said good-naturedly. Kirk got his gun, a double-20-gauge Sterlingworth, from the car. John's gun was a 20-gauge over-and-under, and he surprised Kirk by wearing a holstered pistol. Kirk had not thought John was so much of a weapons man; with a shotgun, why should anyone carry a pistol in the woods? The other two men had pistols as well. None had seemed to be of the type that likes to deck itself with spare guns when going bird hunting.

"Say, Kirk," Gregory said, "you got any rifled slugs for your shotgun?"

"Why, no. Do the grouse get that big up here?"

"You can never tell," Gregory said, with a grin.

"Here, take these pumpkin balls. You got a twenty, ain't you?"

"Yep." Kirk took the shells; they were rifled slugs to fit a 20-gauge shotgun. He put them in the pocket of the light hunting coat he wore over his suit. He wondered why he should take the rifled slugs with him, but no one ventured any explanation, and he decided not to ask. He knew the deer season wasn't open yet.

They walked away from the house with Bumps trailing behind them. Another pointing griffon came tumbling around the house and started after them. Bumps turned and barked twice; the other dog went home. Kirk shook his head. If Gregory was hanging around until he could breed a talking dog, he was pretty near his goal. The group crossed the pasture and climbed the fence at the other side, Kirk being especially careful not to let the barbs catch his suit, though there was very little chance of a barb penetrating it. Gregory looked at him.

"You'd better stay out of the pucker-brush in that outfit, Kirk."

"Pucker-brush?"

"Prickly ash—got sharp, hard thorns on it. I know those suits are tough, but you just might get a rip. You got your patching kit, I guess."

"Yes, sure. But why do they call it pucker-brush?"

Joe Ball laughed and said, "If you got stuck in it without that suit you'd understand."

"Makes your balls pucker up," Greg said. "Okay now, let's get started. Kirk, you take the right wing. If you hear somebody holler *bird,* you look

115

up quick, and don't shoot if it's between you and anybody else. Right?"

"Yes, sir," Kirk said.

"I'll stay in the middle with the dog, and if you hear me say 'Dog's on point,' come on over."

"Right."

"And you two guys, you know what to do. Let's go."

They spread out in a line, perhaps twenty-five yards apart, and started across what had once been an orchard. Kirk found himself tense and excited, wondering what the day was going to bring; he was not anxious to kill, but he was thoroughly enjoying the company of these people and the surroundings. They found nothing in the apple orchard, and beyond were the woods. Kirk found himself in tough going at once; it was a spruce thicket, and the thick dead limbs interlaced in every direction. He was dodging and stooping over and moving along in what he hoped was the proper line. The sun was lost now, but off to his left he could see John's green jacket occasionally. The ground beneath was slick with pine needles. He kept the gun at half-port, a gloved thumb on the safety, the finger within the trigger guard not touching the trigger itself. From far to the left came a sudden distant *whirr!* A sharp *"Bird! Bird!"* A shot, another shot, and a laugh.

"Where did he go, Greg?" John called.

"He didn't go anywhere very much," Greg said. "I missed him on purpose so Joe could get a crack at him."

"Yeah," came Joe's more distant voice. "You sure did."

116

John laughed. Kirk smiled to himself within the helmet. They had gone fifty yards further when suddenly something exploded from somewhere; he didn't know whether it was from bushes, from pine needles or the low branches of a tree. It sounded like an airplane taking off. Kirk stood openmouthed for a moment watching the brown and white blur thrashing away, hitting the little limbs, dodging others. He recovered his wits.

"*Bird, Bird,*" he shouted and threw the shotgun to his shoulder. As he did so, the bird went behind a tree. He pulled the trigger; branches and needles fell. The bird reappeared on the other side, then dodged behind another tree and vanished.

"Shall I send Bumps over to retrieve him?" Greg called.

"Nope, I reckon that won't be necessary," Kirk shouted back, grinning. "No luck."

"What's the matter, Kirk? Can't you hit anything as big and as slow as a grouse?"

Kirk shouted back, "I thought it was an airplane at first; then it stuck a tree between me and it just as I shot."

A laugh came back, and they started forward again. The woods were dull green; the ground was slick, rich brown pine needles. The sun was shining and an occasional dusty-gold-looking beam came down. Mushrooms grew out of the needles, little orange-spotted ones and some large brown-gray ones. Ahead of them the woods thinned and the ground slanted down to a brook; it was only a few inches of water over some black ooze. He climbed up the other side and found himself in an alder swamp. The black alders grew close together, and their leaves were still on. He plunged into gloom spread over dark, slick mud. He fought his way through dead limbs, trees down, branches everywhere, the going getting harder all the time. "How in the name of God could I—?" he thought. Then came the shout again: *"Bird, Bird, Bird,"* and a flapping and a rattling going across in front. He brought the gun to his shoulder, looked ahead, saw the flash of brown in a tiny glade in the distance for only a second. He pulled the trigger anyway, knowing he'd miss by a mile.

"Where did he go?" Greg shouted, and Kirk answered, "Over to the right and ahead."

"Okay, we'll all walk to the right just a little bit, not too much, and maybe we'll walk him up again."

Kirk took a half-turn to the right and walked ahead. It was very quiet except for the distant thrashing sounds that he soon lost. He couldn't see the sun, and everywhere he looked was the same black mud, the same dark, twisted, tangled trunks with yellowing leaves above. He wanted to find that bird again; he wasn't particularly anxious to kill it but he'd like to walk it up again, maybe shove it back over toward the others. He walked rapidly, tearing through the scraping limbs, dodging under, going around, losing his line. He had moved into the shadow of the mountain and he no longer knew the direction in which he was walking. He kept moving for another hundred yards and stopped. He surely should have walked past the bird by now. He listened. There was no sound. He shouted once. Still no sound. He was sure he knew where his friends were. For a moment he thought he heard a shout in the distance, but realized it was a totally different sound. Far off to his right, barely heard, it started with a strange kind of bugle cry, raised to a neigh that had something animal about it, ended almost in a shriek. Then the silence. A chickadee called, "chick-a-dee, dee, dee, chick-a-dee, dee, dee," from close behind him—a familiar little white, gray, and black bird the same size as the chickadees he'd always known. The little fellow was hanging upside down from a limb, pecking away at something. "Chick-a-dee, dee, dee, chick-a-dee, dee, dee." Kirk listened; there was no sound, no bark of a dog. Oh, well, he knew the right way. He was sure of that, for he had a good sense of direction. He turned and started moving in that direction.

Five minutes later he had to admit he didn't know where he was except that he was still in an alder swamp. Here the ground was too hard to take footprints. He began to wonder, uneasily, if he were moving in a circle. He'd let himself get lost. There was nothing to worry about; he didn't think the mountains of Vermont held anything dangerous. Anyway, if he walked downhill long enough he was sure to come to a road. Then the memory of that strange, long cry came back to him. There had been something about it that made the short hairs on the nape of his neck bristle. He wondered what the devil it had been. He thought he heard a shout in a different direction from the one in which he had been going. He started toward it. A little later there was another distant shout, but it was in the wrong direction again, not where the first one had been. Kirk swore to himself. Then he swore aloud. Then he looked all around. Neither the swearing nor the looking around seemed to help. He was a grown man and he knew he was in no danger, but he had to fight very hard to keep the sense of panic, or claustrophobia, from shutting down on him. Everything suddenly seemed sinister, darkening, tough. He felt himself to be in an alien world that had no cause to like him. In the silence of the woods, in the shadows, under trees, behind rocks, there could be nameless things that hated the sound and sight of man. A crow cawed somewhere far away and the chickadee called cheerily close at hand. Kirk had always loved those little birds. Behind him there was a rustle and the crack of a limb. He heard a panting sound, and suddenly Bumps was standing there with him. She sat down, barked once, and started away. Kirk looked at her. My gosh, is she lost, too? She came back and took his glove in her teeth and started pulling him in the direction in which she had started. Kirk knew it was the wrong way. They couldn't possibly be there, but he remembered that Bumps was a smart dog and followed. Ten minutes later he emerged from the swamp, climbed the low, tumbled remnants of a stone wall, went through a birch grove with leaves like gold dollars rustling all around him, and found the other three men seated on rocks in a handsome glade. Gregory was smoking a pipe, Joe a cigarette. John was smiling at him.

"Get yourself a little lost there, Kirk?" Gregory grunted around his pipe.

"Hell, I knew where I was," Kirk grinned. "You guys were the ones that were lost."

"An alder swamp is a kind of funny place sometimes. I see Bumps found you all right. I told her to go bring you over here."

Kirk felt embarrassed. "I thought Bumps was wrong when she started telling me this was the way to go. Then she came back and took me by the hand and started to pull, so I figured maybe I'd better not argue."

"I told you she's got more sense than Greg," Joe said. "Greg gets lost. That's the reason he takes Bumps with him all the time. She'll always take him home."

"Go to hell," grunted Greg around his pipe. He reached into a pocket of his coat and pulled out a handful of gingersnaps and started munching them. They rested a while quietly. Then by common, unspoken consent, they started to walk off again into a small swampy place. There came a soft skittering sound and a whistle. Several birds flew up in darting erratic flight. *Bang!* went a gun. One fell. *Bang!* went another gun. Another fell.

"Woodcock, by God!" shouted Gregory. "Scatter around, boys. We walked these up. We might find some others."

They milled around through the little swamp. They found two more woodcock. One rose straight before Kirk, upward to the right, high, flashing, moving between golden leaves against the gold sky. The gun was at his shoulder; he fired and the woodcock fell with a wisp of feathers floating behind it in the air. Bumps picked up the bird and brought it to him. He held it, small and light, warm and broken in his hand and, though he had hunted and killed before and would do so again, he felt a touch of moisture in his eyes as he looked at the deerlike eyes, closed now, the awkwardly long bill. It was innocence destroyed that he held in his hand, but maybe, he thought, to a worm a woodcock isn't so innocent.

John said, "I see you've got what Ron Trout calls a 'flying liverwurst.' He says they taste like fishing worms."

"I like 'em," said Gregory. "And anybody who doesn't like to eat woodcock can just pass 'em over."

"I don't know whether I like it or not," Kirk said. "But here, you take it, because I don't think that one would go very far. You've got a couple of others to go with it, haven't you?"

"I got two," Greg said. "Joe doesn't like to eat woodcock either. Well, let's get moving." He looked around. "Where the hell is Bumps?"

"She's gone to find a bird for us, I suppose," Joe put in.

Gregory stood and swore picturesquely for a moment, then whistled and called a time or two. "Goddamn that dog," he said.

Joe Ball sat down again.

"What the hell?" Gregory said. "You just going to sit and wait?"

"Sure," Joe said. "I know when I'm well off."

John laughed. Kirk stood puzzled. In a moment there was a rustling in the brush and Bumps came charging out. She sat down in front of Gregory, barked twice, and started back the way she had come.

"Okay, she says we can come now," John said.

Kirk, with the others, followed along behind the dog. She ran up a hillside and came to an opening in the woods. She walked to within ten feet of a brush pile and came to a statuesque point. The four men spread out and walked carefully up to the pile. When they were even with it, Bumps sprang forward, there came a fluttering roar, and three or four grouse flew up in one bursting explosion. Guns shattered the silence. Kirk fired once, missed, fired again, and saw the bird come down. Another bird was down on the other side. Bumps was finding that one. Kirk went ahead, feeling excited. He came up to the large brown-black-white bird lying breast down on the ground, wings beating. Then it was still. He picked it up, big and warm, big as a medium-sized frying chicken. Lovely. Complete, tailored, warm, and dead. He put it in his hunting jacket, wishing he could dry the tears from his face. My God, people would think I'm a softhead, he thought; why do I shoot? He shot because he liked hunting. He shot because of the instinct within him, but it made him a robber to look about the gold and brown woods and realize that they were the poorer for his having been there.

Gregory was growling, "God damn you, Bumps, you go off again and I'll beat hell out of you."

"What's the matter with you, Greg?" Joe said. "She does a good job."

"Sure," Greg growled. "Only when I'm hunting, I want to hunt, I don't want a goddamn mutt bossing the party." Everybody joined in the laughter.

They walked a while longer through the golden autumn woods. The sun was low. A chill was beginning to creep in the shadow beneath a ridge which stretched ahead for a half a mile. Gregory was telling a story about sailing in the Caribbean when he was interrupted; from up on the ridge, perhaps a half a mile away, came the sound that Kirk had heard from the alder swamp: a bugling, rising to a scream—prolonged, equine, a trumpet blast; then silence. The three men with Kirk were perfectly still. Bumps was cowering behind Gregory, shaking.

"What on earth is that?" Kirk said. "I thought I heard it very far away when I was lost in the alder swamp."

"That?" said Gregory. He grinned like a shark. "Oh, that's just a deer."

"I didn't realize they made that kind of noise. Is this the mating season?"

"It's coming up pretty soon," Gregory said. "Yup."

Two chickadees flew by. Kirk noted with a start that these two chickadees were the size of robins, their marking otherwise intact and their song the same. The party came to a mountain orchard, drenched with the fading sunshine of the day. They sat on an old stone wall for a rest and a pipe and a little talking before heading back to Gregory's house. Red apples lay on the ground, more dangled from the trees of the abandoned orchard. Gregory picked several and took a bite of one.

"Man, that's good," he said. "Kirk, I don't feel much like Eve, and maybe I don't look like her, but here, have an apple."

Kirk caught it in his gloved hand. He was taking his fifteen-minute budget time. He had had a sandwich in his pocket and had just finished eating that. He stirred uneasily; this was a radiated apple.

It had not been deradded. It was wild. It had grown as an apple should grow. It had not had its cells changed around by the deradder to remove the radiation from it. It was smooth and gleaming and had little green and brown speckles on it, and looked healthy and beautiful. It was a thing that grew wild to be eaten by the deer, to be pecked by grouse, to be taken by the animals of nature. Not exactly knowing what impelled him, realizing it was foolish ever to eat radiated food, Kirk took a bite. Maybe because it was forbidden, maybe because of the day, maybe because of a hundred things—the smell of the woods, of pine needles, dying leaves, the smell of autumn—Kirk thought that never in his life had anything tasted as delicious as that apple. A thrill ran through him; behind the bite and the taste came a longing so sharp that it shook him as he sat on the stone wall. Oh, my God! he thought. If it could be as it used to be! If this world could be untouched and unruined by man! If mankind had been less greedy, or if man had never interpreted that word in the Bible to mean he could destroy all around him without compunction. Oh, if things could only be as they might have been! His thoughts were so intent, so full of anguish that he was surprised that the others didn't hear him groan aloud. He let the half-eaten apple fall to the ground and tried to smile.

Alone in his room that night, Kirk did something he hadn't done in a long time. He sat before his desk, pulled the light to him, and placed his left hand beneath it, searching for the R. He knew that the reactive material that was placed within the hand of every human being was there. It was there for the protection of the individual, a constant, reliable warning to indicate if he had somehow absorbed too much radiation. Even Normal country had a radiation background much higher than had been the case before, and it accumulated bit by bit. He turned off the light, and in the darkness placed his hand before his eyes and stared. No glimmer of orange. He turned the black light on his hand. No R.

The Rs on other people no longer bothered Kirk, except that the one on Anne's hand filled him with sorrow and anguish because they were so thoroughly walled apart. He was not a Robertist. He loved one of them and admired others, but he didn't want to become one. That would be the end of a normal, unencumbered life in Normal country. His career would be cut short. He would never again be more than a technician, working in a plant and wearing a suit there. He would wear a suit when visiting his parents. He would become an underprivileged citizen. Originally the position of a Robert had not been thought of as being less good than that of Normals. It had been a matter of health and precaution, at first, but he knew it was becoming more than that now. If only, he thought, if only, dear God! there was some way that Anne could be made clean! Clean!—he ground his teeth in anger at the thought. The thoughtless expressions, the things that were said. You were clean if you were not radiated. Therefore you were dirty if you were not clean. Anne, therefore, was dirty. Dear God, he thought, that's the way the thinking begins. That is the thing that's going to split the human race apart. He sat filled with long thoughts and despair until it came time for him to take his shift. He could hardly wait to see Anne again, for when he was with her he forgot these things.

Two days later George Sneck called Kirk into his office again.

"In a hurry, Kirk?" the superintendent asked.

"Why?" Kirk asked. "Yes, I was going up to town."

"I suppose you're going to see your Robert friends?"

"That's right," Kirk said, nettled. "I certainly am. I have met some wonderful people here, and I thoroughly enjoy being with them. Is there any objection?"

"Cool down, son," George Sneck said, leaning back in his chair. "I'm talking to you for your own good. It's a good thing for the company and the plant for you to have friends among the Roberts. It's a good precaution. You can let us know if anything ever starts cooking among them. I haven't got anything against Roberts. Why, some of my best friends are Roberts. But don't you go fraternizing too much, young man."

"Isn't that my business, sir?" Kirk said.

"Well, yes, it is, up to a point, but not after too much fraternizing. You'll keep slipping a little bit here and a little bit there and the first thing you know you're gonna have your R show. Don't let your R show, boy," he said. "Think what it would be like to be a Robert. All I gotta do, young fellow, is to send in a report on you saying that you are seeing too much of the Roberts, that you're in danger of getting dirty."

Kirk ground his teeth.

"And also that you seem to be not showing the attitude proper for a powerman in the VPC. You'd be home right soon, I guess, young man, and then you'd be out again, somewhere in Greenland or the Arctic or the Antarctic. Somewhere where there wouldn't be any Roberts around for you to play with. I'm just talking for your own good, young fellow. I like you, I like the cut of your jib. I think you've got the makings of a good man. Now, I don't say you shouldn't see your friends, you go right ahead and see them, but just mind what I have said. I can get you out of here anytime. And another thing. This guy Martin you see all the time, the college professor. There's a couple things I don't like about him—now, don't go heating up, young fellow, or maybe I'll send you south right now. I say there's things I don't like about Martin. One is he's a professor; another thing is, he worries too much about animals and birds and such. I've heard him talk. But the worst thing is, his electric bill is too low."

"Oh, come on, Mr. Sneck. You can't hold that against a man!"

"The hell I can't. He's bootlegging power some way. I've had the meter checked, and he's not screwing it up. It's something else, and I bet I know what it is."

"What?"

"Never you mind. When I find out, I'll burn his rear end for him. But that's none of your business. You had better mind what I say, or I'll ship you out. Do you understand?"

"Yes, sir, I understand," Kirk said. "But I don't like it."

"It's for your own good, son, and so long as you understand it, I reckon it don't make a hell of a lot of difference whether you like it or not. All right, you can go now."

Kirk went out of the room. He had never before felt the anger seething within him that he felt now. He felt a rebellion growing within himself. Anne, dirty! Don't let your R show! He went back to his room, got into his suit, and headed for his electric car and Waybury.

Chapter Six /

FAREWELL INNOCENCE

During all that October, Kirk Patrick lived a double love affair, one with the land and one with Anne.

By mid-October the mountains, fields, and woods had reached an almost unbelievable peak of loveliness. Hardly the most insensitive Vermont oldtimer could be unmoved by the spectacle, even though he had lived with it during all the autumns of his life. Many of the sugar maples had turned a red that seemed to burn itself, a crimson heat against the blue sky and the gold of the yellow maples, the bronze of the oaks, the dark green of evergreens, the white shafts of birches supporting leaves that were nebulae of golden coins. Kirk was made glad by the beauty, partially because it was the strongest possible proof of a guiding and creative intelligence. The earth about him was obviously a beautiful, complex work of the highest art, which could be no accident. The creation of art is an act of intelligence. For God's sake, Kirk grumbled to himself at these thoughts. A little bit more of this and they can stick you up with Spade, Mop, and Goat and let you teach philosophy.

These thoughts passed through his mind as he

was driving in to pick up Anne. They were going to call on Gregory and Liz on the mountain top. Kirk had come to like Gregory very much, valuing the stubborn independence about him that maintained the integrity of the individual against all comers. He picked up Anne at John's house and John waved at them from the carport as they left. Diana was upended in a flower bed as usual. As they drove toward the mountains they found many cars on the highway, most with the license plates of Normal country.

"Leaf lookers," Anne said with a smile.

"They've got something to look at this year," Kirk said.

"Isn't it gorgeous?"

"Yes. I was just thinking a while ago that looking at it makes me believe in God."

"Why, Kirk," Anne said, "I didn't think you Normals believed in God any more."

"I don't know, a lot of them say they do. I've always been an agnostic, but somehow since I've come to Vermont I'm beginning to believe."

"Yes," Anne said soberly, "but I wish He hadn't let us play with our toys so freely. It must take a strange kind of God to let a lot of untamed, untrained idiot brats mess up His masterpiece."

"Maybe it is not His masterpiece," he said gently. "Maybe this earth was just a little tryout, a little primitive art work, one that could be turned over to a group of unruly children who won't learn."

"Right now," Anne said, "I'm happy. I don't want to think serious and somber thoughts."

"Wonderful! Me too!"

"Good."

"Now what'll we talk about?"

They talked about the children in Anne's room and that conversation, too, began to be tinged with sadness, and they switched again, determinedly. This time about Gregory and Liz.

"He's a character," Anne said. "He's one of the most amazing men I've ever met, and Liz is right up with him. You'll find out today, if you talk to them about it, that Gregory is a great sailor. They used to go every summer and cruise the Caribbean."

Several times they encountered cars filled with men who were wearing orange or red hats and coats. Mostly Normals, it seemed. Two cars passed them, tooting raucously into the silence as they did so.

"Surely they don't have to wear those red clothes to look at leaves?" Kirk said.

"Oh, dear, I'd forgotten about that!" Anne said. "Gregory might be a little peppery today. I never remember the early deer season; there've gotten to be so many deer in Vermont that for the last three years now, the Fish and Game Department has started deer season in the middle of October. I believe they thought that people would like to hunt more and would enjoy it more with all the color in the hills. But I sometimes wonder if these deer hunters ever notice the foliage."

"I do," Kirk said. "And you know I like to hunt."

"I know, so does Dad. But when he hunts he sees every tree and leaf and all the things around him. I don't think he really cares to bring home much game. Oh, he likes to have a grouse or a duck, and he's gotten a couple of deer. But I think he shoots mostly to complete the function of hunting."

"That's exactly the way I feel," Kirk said. "I admire your father very much."

"Thank you," Anne said. "He seems to like you too. I can't quite understand it, of course." She smiled at him.

Greg and Liz's house on the mountainside looked out on a breathtaking amphitheater of color. Far away the sun glinted on the ribbon of Lake Champlain in its veil of vapor; beyond that the Adirondacks glowed. Beauty was all about, and the air was like a beneficent wish to man.

The Mainyards greeted them happily and took them for a tour of Greg's garden plot and to see the horses, sheep, and cows. Greg was a picture of the old farmer with boots and mustache and gray hair, deep-set eyes twinkling. Liz was lively and youthful still, sparring with him verbally, undisturbed by his raucous comments. Greg was just describing an incident of their last cruise in Maine when they were interrupted. A large car turned in the driveway and came speeding up, throwing gravel on the curves.

"Who the bloody hell is that?" Greg exclaimed. "Don't they see that private driveway sign down there?"

"It's deer season, Greg," Liz said.

"Oh, Christ. I'd forgotten. It doesn't seem right to go deer hunting in October, and I'll be damned if I'll do it. I'll wait till November when all these damn leaves are off the damn trees. Now what the hell do these people want?" Greg strode forward to stand by the road.

Kirk walked forward, a little bit to the rear, as support in whatever encounter might ensue.

Men piled out of the car. All but one were Normals wearing the transparent suits; beneath the suits they were gaudy. Pants, shirts and caps were of brilliant red or a harsh, clashing orange that caught the eye and held it. They were the electric colors, the neon colors, Kirk thought; against the natural colors of the forest they stood out like harsh, unshaded electric lights. Each man carried a shiny rifle, and each man was encircled by a cartridge belt from which dangled a pistol, an enormous hunting knife, and, in a couple of cases, a coil of light line. They were going to drag the deer with those. A gaunt, stooped Robert with faded blue eyes and straggly whiskers was the last out of the car. He came up to Gregory.

"Mr. Mainyard, those fellows want to hunt some deer and they've paid me to guide 'em. I was wondering could we pass across your wood lot and into the National Forest land? They won't shoot on your land at all."

Liz and Anne had come up to the group, too. Liz looked worried.

"Now, Gregory," she said soothingly.

Gregory's face was red as he started to speak. One of the red-coated hunters spoke first. He had the well-nourished pink face and manicured look of a successful Normal businessman. He selected Gregory as the target.

"We'll pay you for the privilege, Jack," he said.

"What the hell, we'll give you twenty bucks if we can just leave the car here and cross your land."

Another of the hunters said, in an aside to a third hunter easily heard by all present, "Gad, what a typical Vermonter!"

"What do you say, Jack?" asked the first. "We won't hurt your land. Twenty dollars ain't hay. You couldn't charge a man that much for hauling his car out of a ditch." He laughed.

Gregory grew redder, bit his moustache, and looked down at the ground.

"Have you hunted deer around here before?" Gregory asked the faded man in chin whiskers, the Robert who, unlike the others, was wearing a weathered old brown hunting coat.

"Ayuh. Reckon I was shootin' deer around here before you was, Mister Mainyard. I know these woods and these deer. I was born and raised in Ripton; I been away for a while, but I ain't forgot the country."

Gregory nodded and looked over at the leader of the four Normals.

"Are you men sure you can take care of yourselves in the woods?" he asked quietly.

"Don't worry about us, Jack," the man replied with a laugh. "We've got compasses, maps, and a guide. We don't need you for another guide—this specimen is more than enough. God, you Roberts really like to make a dollar, don't you?"

Liz's hair turned a shade redder, and she started to speak: "Why, you half—"

"Shh, Liz," Gregory said, very quietly.

"It's none of my business," he went on. "But have

136

you heard anything about deer attacking hunters?
They can be mean."

The four Norms laughed; one nudged another.
"That old buzzard," the leader said, indicating the
Robert guide, "said something about deer turning
mean. That's a lot of crap. If they do, we're ready
for them."

"I guess the radiation goes to the Roberts' heads
too," another hunter said.

"It sure goes to their guts," another replied.
"Scared of deer. That really takes the cake. Come
on, let's go."

"Are you going to let us cross your land or not?"
the first Norm demanded. "We haven't got all day
to stand here talking with you."

"You'd better not wear those clothes," Gregory
said, looking at the brilliant red and orange hunting outfits.

"Oh, for God's sake!" the leader was disgusted.
"What are you Roberts trying to give us? What's
wrong with these clothes? You want us to shoot
one another, I guess. Listen, Jack, we know what
we're doing."

"They're just trying to keep us out of the woods,
Paul," a second Norm said contemptuously.

"I think you're right. Look, Jack, we've got just
as much right in the National Forest as anybody
else. Now, do you want to make twenty bucks by
letting us leave our car here and cross your land, or
don't you? We can find another place, you know."

Gregory grinned like a shark.

"Help yourselves, gents, and have a good hunt.
Pull your car off the road down by the barn where
it will be out of the way, and don't shoot no cows."

"That's more like it. Here's your twenty. See, Jack, not all Normals are suckers, the way you Roberts seem to think. Come on, boys, let's get going."

A few minutes later the hunters vanished across the orchard, their red or orange coats shining like beacons in the clear day.

"Gregory," said Liz. "Do you think you should?"

"Should what? Let them cross our land? Why not? They won't hurt it."

"But I don't think the man with them knows what he's doing. Do they know about the deer?"

"He says he does, and about the country too. And you heard me warn 'em. Other people have warned them too. I even told them about their clothes—they're just too smart to listen. They said they could take care of themselves. My God, I should think they could. They've got artillery enough to handle all the deer in the woods."

"But do they know about the wolverdeer?"

"Had a Robert with 'em. He ought to know. To hell with them. I warned them, and I let them cross my land. Now I don't want to talk about it anymore."

They stood in the golden sunshine looking at the world of color about them for a little longer, and then went into the house. Liz had agreed to show some slides they had taken in the Caribbean on a sailing cruise. Kirk had done some sailing; not much, but enough so he could appreciate and enjoy the pictures and the Gregory-Liz comments which went with them. Perhaps an hour had passed when Gregory stopped in midstory and raised a hand.

"Wait. Thought I heard a shot." He got up and started outside, Liz right behind him. Anne looked worried. Kirk caught her eye, and they followed the others.

"I guess they found a deer," Gregory said. "I'm sure I heard a shot."

They listened in the quiet afternoon. A crow cawed overhead, and in the distance a jay shouted raucously. Kirk turned up the volume on his suit, and he could hear the others breathing, and the sigh of the gentle wind. Bumps whined behind them.

A rifle shot cracked, sounding as if it were a mile or so away. Gregory's face was hard as iron. Liz whispered something. All four of them stared up the mountain in the direction of the shot, and a nameless dread stole over Kirk. He felt Anne's hand on his glove; he saw that Gregory's moustache seemed to bristle.

Then came a shot, then another, then several together. Kirk heard the faint, far-off echo of a cry, then a yell, sounding like a scream. Even at this distance the vibrations of terror could be heard in that cry. Then came the sound Kirk had heard in the alder swamp, on the grouse hunt; a swelling, bugling shriek, rising, falling, inhuman, animal! He could feel the hairs on his neck bristling, and fear gripped him. Immediately it was followed by another hair-raising call from a different direction.

"Two of them!" Liz cried. Anne's face was white. "Oh, Gregory," Liz went on frantically. "You've got to do something!"

"Can you shoot a rifle?" Gregory asked Kirk.

"Yes."

"Do you want to help those guys out? See if we can save any of them?"

"My God, yes, of course! What *is* it?"

Anne was looking at Kirk, her face even whiter, her eyes enormous. Kirk suddenly felt very brave, even though he was frightened by the unknown something.

"Come on!" Greg said, leading the way into the house. He opened a closet and handed Kirk a holstered revolver. "This is a magnum 357. This will stop them, if you can hit 'em with it." He took out a rifle, a pump gun. "This is a thirty-thirty. There's one in the chamber and six in the magazine. Here are some extra shells. Can't tell how many we'll need." Kirk fumbled the handful of shells into his outer pocket, belted on the pistol, and picked up the rifle.

"I'm coming too!" cried Liz.

"Like hell. You and Anne stay here, in the house, you hear me? Keep your rifle handy."

"Oh, Kirk, do be careful!" Anne cried, her voice trembling, her hand on his suited arm. He smiled at her, though his lips felt stiff. Unknown danger is the most terrifying of all.

Then they were out of the door, closing it behind them on Anne and Liz and the dogs and on the security of the solid house, and running into the flaming October woods. They hit a fast clip going through the orchard and up the mountainside. Gregory's long, leathery frame was tough as steel. Kirk was soon panting, but Greg's breathing was even and he spoke around the pipe in his mouth.

"We don't talk much about this to strangers, and I guess you've noticed that. We don't like to talk or think about it at all. You're not a stranger now, but it never occurred to me to tell you about it. I thought probably John had. Those things you heard screaming are deer."

"*Deer?*" exclaimed Kirk, panting.

"Yes, just plain ordinary deer physically, but you know this radiation we've been exposed to for so long? Things in the natural world, animals, birds, insects, particularly the species that have a new generation every year, have changed, mutated. They are often different from what they used to be, and it's something that is going to continue at an increased rate."

"Yes," said Kirk. "I've wondered about that."

"Some pretty smart scientists," Gregory said as they dodged into the edge of the woods, "think that that is what happened to create man. Through some nova exploding somewhere in space, the earth was bathed in increased radiation for an appreciable period of time. That increased radiation made some creature, an ape, a monkey, something, change, made its brain grow. They think that radiation is behind all evolutionary change. The changes that are good, that work, make the changed animal live and transmit its characteristics; the changes that don't work cause the species to die off. Well, some of the deer have mutated. They're still herbivorous, not carnivorous. We thought they were meat eaters for a while, but they're not. Certain deer, mostly bucks but some does as well, have developed vicious fighting instincts. We call them wolverdeer because they act like wolverines. Leave a wolverine alone and he'll leave you alone; mess with him and he comes at you. And these deer do just that."

"They haven't got teeth, have they? I mean, you know, the kind of teeth that are dangerous?"

"Teeth? Hell, what do they need with teeth? The bucks have horns and hooves, the does hooves, and they can cut you to ribbons, and fast, man! It's like taking a quick wing shot when you shoot at one of them. You've seen a deer run away in a hurry, but wait until you see one running *after* you! They go twenty, thirty feet at a jump, *fast* and hard as hell to hit. They never stop; they go after you with horns and hooves, they're not afraid, and they come at you until the're dead. You've got to kill 'em to stop 'em. They have developed a trait of deadly, vicious fighting, offensive fighting if they're bothered, and they also have developed a trait of being infuriated instantly by anyone dressed in brightly colored clothes, especially red or bright orange. You see, hunters have been wearing these colors over a good number of years, and the deer have come to associate them with being attacked."

They stopped a moment to listen.

"If a man shoots a doe out of a wolverdeer's herd, that wolverdeer attacks instantly, and he won't quit until you or he, one, is dead. Or if he's lost a doe, or been shot at himself, he'll attack any man he sees. But if you're not bothering him or his herd, and if you're not wearing orange or red, or some other really bright color, and if he hasn't been wounded or lost any does recently, he won't bother you. If they get the sight or scent of man they'll turn away and go up into the woods. That's why you can hunt or walk in the woods a long time and never see one. We carry rifled slugs and a pistol when we grouse hunt—somebody might have annoyed a wolverdeer. There aren't many of them. So far, only a small percentage has mutated into wolverdeer."

"God!" Kirk exclaimed. "That's awful! Why isn't it known?"

"A recent development," Gregory growled. "We haven't reported it for a couple of reasons. The state doesn't want to lose out on the income from out of state hunting licenses; it needs the money to try to take care of people. And they think that if the goddamn federal government found out about it, it would send Wildlife Service hunters up here with helicopters, machine guns, and poison and eliminate the wolverdeer. The only way to do it would be to kill off the whole deer herd, and we won't stand for that. Come on; we've got to get moving faster. Some of those guys are probably in serious trouble up there."

A flurry of shots sounded ahead. Kirk heard more terror-stricken yells, and he saw a glint of bright red coming through the woods. Two men burst into a cleared space. One was the Robert guide. He was in front, unhindered by a suit. Behind him was one of the hunters. Another man was screaming up on the mountain. The howl of a wolverdeer cut through the afternoon, raising Kirk's hair, turning his stomach cold and contracted, making his hands shake, his eyes blur. Then he saw a swift, bounding brown shape whistling through the air in leaps that took it twenty or thirty feet at a time, a brown streak flashing through the woods. A deer, but such a deer! Head outstretched, neck level, brown hair bristling, screaming harshly! Gregory fired beside Kirk. Kirk threw up his rifle, fumbled off the safety, caught the brown streak over his sights and squeezed off a shot. Missed! He pumped, squeezed off again. Missed! Gregory fired. They both fired together, and the brown thing was hit at the top of a leap. It crashed to earth, rolled, thrashed, was on its feet, screaming. It leaped again, and its horns skewered the running man, pinning him to the ground. The small hooves flashed as they tore the man's suit and body. Kirk steadied himself and fired. The deer dropped, then tried to get up again. Gregory fired, and down it went to lie still. There came a crashing from the right, another scream. Gregory fired and shouted:

"To your right, to your right!"

Kirk saw coming at them, straight at them, them alone, another deer. Horns spread wide, head down, charging, leaping, flashing at him! Kirk shot and shot again. Gregory was shooting beside him. The wolverdeer's legs went out from under it, it fell on its head, turned a complete somersault, landed ten feet away, and started struggling to its feet. Kirk was almost reduced to sheer impotence, complete inaction, by the flaming red of its eyes, the bared equine teeth, the blood, the sharp hooves. Its hindquarters wouldn't move. Back broken, partially paralyzed, it dragged itself toward them by its front hooves, screaming. Gregory shot again. Kirk forced himself to cover the head with his sights and squeezed the trigger, firing his last cartridge. The deer slumped to earth, front legs still moving even as its red eyes closed. The animal's dying lunge inched it a little closer to Kirk.

Kirk staggered back. He unzipped his helmet and lurched over, vomiting, sick, shaking, cold, then hot. He felt Gregory's hand on his suited shoulder.

"All right, Kirk, it's all right. All over."

Gregory threatened to shoot the guide if he didn't go up the mountain with them. The man skewered by the deer was stone dead, but some of the others might still be alive. Up on the ridge, in a forest that felt totally alien to Kirk, they found a young spikehorn, dead—the animal first shot by the hunters. Fifty feet away they found the body of the leading hunter, a fearful sight. Not far away was another hunter. He wasn't quite dead, but he died as they tried to turn him over.

They found the fourth hunter across the little glade, untouched but dead, his face purple, eyes staring.

"Heart attack, I think," Gregory said, grimly. "A stroke maybe."

"I don't blame him," Kirk said, weakly.

The flaming woods were perfectly quiet now. In Kirk rose a steady horror, a cold disillusionment, a feeling of terrible loss. Bambi, the gentle deer, the gentle animal, had changed into this flashing, red-eyed demon. Innocent no more. Mankind, through greed and utter selfishness, had aroused these things, and now mankind was going to be coping with them more and more. Not just the wolverdeer, not just here, this was only the beginning. A cold fear for the human race shut down on Kirk—who knew what changes were taking place in man himself? He remembered Yeats: "And what rough beast . . . Slouches towards Bethlehem to be born?"

They sent for the police, game wardens, and forest rangers who carried out the dead. The car was driven away. The questioning was over. Kirk found himself shaking and still clutched in the cold dread, even as he looked about him at the glorious wonder of the day that man had polluted.

"Come in and have a drink, Kirk," Gregory said. "I want to tell you, you're a man. It takes a man to stand up in front of one of those wolverdeer and shoot till the thing drops. I saw you shooting and you were hitting. Put her there, boy." He held out a horny hand and Kirk grasped it with his gloved one. They went into the house before the fireplace where a great log burned and a black kettle simmered with some sort of stew above it. Gregory liked game stew cooked over an open fire. Kirk took budget time; he went beyond his budget for a full half hour this time. All four of them had two glasses of rum with a little ginger ale mixed with it. Anne was still very pale, and every time she looked at Kirk something in her eyes made him feel eight feet tall.

Gregory said, "Goddamn it, Kirk, I'm sorry we had to shoot those wolverdeer. I admire them. I think that's the way a man ought to be. Don't bother anybody if they don't bother you, but if they attack you, wipe 'em out! I think there are going to be more and more of them all the time, Kirk. Not just the deer, other things as well."

Kirk repressed a shudder. He remembered the woods, the world—the wildlife so long inoffensive, so harmless to man, living within its own enclosed world. He thought of the flashing courage of those deer, charging still as they died. He remembered the gross and loud men who had hunted them. He reached out and touched Anne's hand.

"I hope so," he said.

Chapter Seven /

DEAD CREEK

Time passed, and as the color faded from the October woods into the grayness of November, the horrible memories of the wolverdeer incident faded from Kirk's mind. He had expected great commotion over the affair, but after some careful questioning of himself, Gregory, and the Robert guide, he and Gregory had simply been thanked for their services. Most of the incident dropped from public notice. The Burlington *Free Press* noted in a story somewhere inside that a bizarre hunting accident had resulted in the accidental death of three out-of-state hunters, and the natural death of a fourth from a heart attack. Kirk's part in the affair was not made public, and he did not tell his associates at the plant about it.

He had expected that he would feel a horror of the woods, but only a few days later he went grouse hunting with John and Gregory and found that the enchantment was still there. Now he understood the rifled slugs that his friends always carried and insisted that he carry as well, and the magnum revolvers. He secured a 357 magnum Smith and Wesson of his own. He did not want to be caught defenseless against such an onslaught as he had witnessed. Gregory and John had assured him that attacks by the wolverdeer on humans were very rare; a person in the woods not dressed in hunter's colors, not bothering deer, was not likely to be attacked. Of course, Gregory had said, "If you meet up with one that's been hit or hurt, or that's lost a doe, or has been hunted hard recently, he just might take out after you. That's why we always carry a magnum when we go into the woods even for a walk; if you learn to shoot it then you should be safe. You hit him anywhere with that magnum and it will knock him down."

One Sunday Kirk took Anne to church. The preacher, a Robert, moderately sized, young and redheaded, radiated a quiet warmth and cheerfulness; he spoke and officiated well. Obviously the liturgy meant a great deal to him and to the people in the church, certainly to Anne. She no longer looked sad. Morning prayers were read; the chants, hymns, all these things seemed to create a feeling of warmth, of refuge and serenity in the church. Kirk felt it strongly. The reason, he supposed, was that the Reverend Stephen White was using the old prayer book. The beauty of the language warmed and delighted Kirk, archaic though it was. Perhaps, as people had said, it obscured meaning, but poetry was there, and beauty, and it certainly did not obscure the meaning for him. He thought of the sentence the preacher had just spoken, ending the Gospel for that day. *Jesus preached to his disciples and departed from them.* Kirk turned the sentence over in his mind, thinking of its rhythm, thinking of its air of serenity and leisure. He compared it with the same phrase from the new Third

Revised Standard Bible which was in universal use in Normal country: *Jesus rapped with his cats and split*. The new version was crisper, there was no doubt about it. It was brief, and it carried an impact for so slight a sentence. Somehow, though, the language of the old prayer book was better for him. He shook hands with the preacher afterwards and told him that he had enjoyed the service.

"Good," Stephen White said, "I hope that you'll come back often, Mr. Patrick. We have a number of Normals from the college in our congregation, as you have noticed. So I trust that you will feel no awkwardness in coming here."

"Of course not, sir," Kirk said. He laughed. "As a matter of fact, I find myself forgetting that I wear a suit."

"Very nice to see you, Anne. Are you coming to the parish supper next week?" Anne was coming to the parish supper and they discussed it a moment and then Anne and Kirk walked off into the November day.

The land was waiting now. It had been a long warm fall. The first frost had come and gone. The grass was crisp and ceasing to grow in John Martin's yard. The flowers were gone except for the full bronzes and yellows of the chrysanthemums, and they were beginning to look somewhat worn. The woods were gray and black, and beech and birch trunks shone through the November air like candles. Brown leaves were piled so deeply in the woods that squirrels dashing through the leaves sounded like deer. When Kirk and Anne walked up Snake Mountain one day, they waded knee-deep through the brown, rustling piles. At night a few insects cried with a monotonous chirping, faint now. To Kirk there was a sound of sadness, of resignation, in their songs. He was sure that, not consciously, but somehow through the generations of their strange, remote race, they knew that the end of their lives lay close. In the winter the nights would be silent, and only when the snow was gone would the peepers' silver croak be heard again.

Duck season was open, and the first fervor of the blood hunters was over. The people who went out in swarms on opening days and slaughtered the ducks not yet accustomed to the fact that another hunting season had arrived had performed their ritual and gone. The winds were cold, bitter rains fell, and already there were snow flurries in the mountains.

"Say, Kirk," John said, "can you get off tomorrow afternoon? We might go out to Dead Creek and try to frog us up a few ducks."

"I'd love that, sir," Kirk said.

"All right, good. Why don't you come by about, oh, right after your lunch. We'll be there about two o'clock, and stay until after sunset."

* * *

"Off again with your pet Roberts, Patrick?" George Sneck asked him the next day as they met in the yard.

Kirk was already suited up and headed for the garage. "I certainly am going out with one of my Robert friends," he said. "I wouldn't exactly call Professor Martin a pet."

"What is it this time?" Sneck asked. "Strolling in the woods? Not very pretty weather for it."

"Duck hunting," Kirk said shortly.

"I see. Okay, I'll be seeing you, Kirk."

Kirk looked after the man as he walked away. The supervisor had sounded rather serious. Kirk had realized that there was some talk at the power station about his spending so much of his free time among the Roberts. Well, he had to live his own life; he was following all the rules, and he knew he was doing a good job at the station. He shrugged and walked on to his car. He had lunch at the normalized dining room of the Midway Inn and went by for John at one o'clock. Anne was busy in her school.

The day was cold. Kirk, locked in his suit, felt none of it. A thin, cold rain fell, blowing in the wind, but not heavily enough to obscure the mountains. The clouds were just above the mountain tops. Wood smoke curled from John's chimney. Kirk knocked at the front door, wiped his feet with extreme care on the mat outside, and went in when he heard the invitation of Diana's voice. He found her in the living room, knitting before a warm, quiet fire. The wind whined in the chimney and rain spattered against the windows. She looked at him and smiled.

"John's downstairs getting his boots on. Why don't you just go down—you'll find him in the study. I must say I think you're both idiots to go out on a day like this."

"You've got to be crazy to be a duck hunter, Diana," Kirk said. He had become very fond of this woman. She was handsome, always doing some-

153

thing, and usually cheerful; she exhibited toward her easygoing, sometimes somewhat fumbling husband an exasperated warm affection and a total loyalty. Kirk had often thought that the two together were the most complete complements of one another of any couple he had ever known. He grinned at her again. She snuggled a little closer before the fire and he went downstairs. He found John in his hip boots.

"Afternoon, Kirk," he said. "This is a beautiful day, isn't it?"

You did have to be crazy to be a duck hunter, Kirk thought, because John really meant it. Another gust of wind blew rain against the study windows. It was a disheveled, messed up room with a wall of books and a typing table and comfortable chairs, books everywhere and papers scattered all over.

"This place drives Diana frantic," John said. "It looks terrible, I guess, but I know where everything is and I can find it." He shrugged into a camouflaged hunting coat. "There's one thing I like about the early deer season," he said. "By the time you get to good duck weather like this, deer season's over and done with, and you don't have to worry about getting shot going back to your car. You know how some of those birds hunt deer, don't you? They drive along the country roads in cars—their rifles aren't supposed to be loaded, but it's pretty hard to check them all. They park in the late afternoon by a field or wood and wait, hoping that a deer will come out in the last light to feed. Then they will kill him without ever getting their asses off the soft seat cushions."

"That's not hunting," Kirk said indignantly. "Nothing but slaughter. We don't have to worry about that today. Nothing but those lovely ducks."

After half an hour's driving, John pulled off into an empty graveled parking lot on the edge of a brown and silver marsh. "Good!" John exclaimed. "I was hoping no one would beat us to it. Do you know this kind of duck hunting, Kirk?"

"No, sir. My duck hunting has been in a blind."

"We call it frogging. We walk along close to the edge of the marsh. The ducks fly up out of the reeds and we take a pop at them. They're harder to hit than a grouse when they take off like that suddenly and you don't see them leave the water."

In an area perhaps ten to twelve miles long, roller dams had been constructed on Dead Creek, backing up the water so that a long, winding stretch of marsh had been made. It reached back into sloughs and coves and small tributary streams. It was an ideal duck breeding, feeding, and resting area. The rich brown of cattails and reeds showed everywhere; sometimes patches of alders still survived toughly and offered brambled black entanglements in which a duck was safe from anything. John and Kirk crossed over the small fence that prevented cars from driving down this side of the creek, and were within an area where hunting was legal. John stopped and looked about him. Kirk followed his example, beginning to feel the charm of the scene and the day. Rain whipped against his helmet and he cursed, hoping the rain would slacken off. He was warm and dry, but the water on the front of the helmet made it hard to see properly. Large level fields and meadows, brown now, lay between him and Snake Mountain. Trees grew in the fence rows, occasional solitary trees in the fields, and pine groves looked dark in the rain. The water of the Dead Creek preserve was dark, ruffled in the wind, and bare-limbed trees poked gaunt arms against the gray sky. It was a cold scene and an elemental one.

John lit his pipe, putting it in his mouth upside down. The burnt ashes fell to the ground as they were consumed, while the packed tobacco remained in the pipe, undampened by the rain. His brown, somewhat round face was cheerful and pleased as he looked at Kirk and grinned.

"Most people who hunt here like this bring a retriever dog along, because usually if you do get a duck he falls into the water."

"I see," Kirk said. "But we haven't got a dog."

"No," said John. "We haven't got a dog, have we, Kirk."

"I don't get it," Kirk said.

"Ah, but I hope you will. Some people bring dogs for retrievers. Others—ah—bring—ah—Norms, you know. In that nice suit of yours, why you can wade right out up to your chin, pretty nearly. Can't you, boy?"

Kirk looked at him, shook his head, then barked ingratiatingly.

"Heel, boy," John said, and, laughing, they walked along the edge of the water, finding a pathway near the brink with tall reeds growing above their heads at the edges of the water. Black-gray sky was above them and grassy, weedy bank to the left. The rain slacked off now, and Kirk wiped his

156

helmet clear with an absorbent cloth he carried in an outer access pocket. For convenience he was wearing his hunting coat on top of the suit.

"Freeze!" John said suddenly. "Here come some teal."

Kirk didn't move a muscle.

"Look to the right, coming downwind! Man! Are they traveling! Get ready."

Kirk saw the little cloud of ducks, a dozen perhaps, flashing fairly low over the water and the reeds, close in. They would pass within range.

"All set," John said. "All set, don't move. Hold still. Okay, now!"

Kirk whirled. The ducks were just coming. They'd be even with them in another moment. With the wind behind them and their natural speed, they were making a terrific speed. The gun went to his shoulder automatically. He looked down the barrel at one of the ducks, swung the barrel far ahead, fired, and nothing happened. He swung it ahead of another duck, farther this time, and fired again. Nothing happened. He heard John's gun go off as his first shot was fired, and John fired again shortly after Kirk had emptied his second barrel. The teal kept right on going.

"Good trip, boys!" John shouted at them, and turned back to Kirk with a grin. "It doesn't look like the two of us are going to slaughter many ducks, does it, son? Well, that's all right with me. Aren't they beauties, though? Don't those little fellows move?"

"Yes, sir."

"They aren't much bigger than a bumble bee,"

John said, "but they sure are sweet and tasty in the pan. Even deradded they're still good."

They took it easy and slow, talking quietly, laughing softly, enjoying the harshness of the November day, omen of the weather soon to come. It folded them in, making them a part of the quiet scene with its low-pitched colors, rich brown, black, gray, silver, and the cattails waving in the icy wind. Kirk found himself thinking that he would rather be here at this moment than any other place on earth. He *was* crazy after all.

A squawk, a spattering of water, a beating of wings against reeds, forty yards ahead, close to shore; then some big, dark-looking birds surged upward, squawking again.

"Mallards," shouted John.

Kirk found his gun at his shoulder. Hardly having time to aim, he fired. He saw one of the birds go into a somersault and drop heavily with a splash. John fired a second time and another duck slanted, wings flailing, down into the water. The four survivors, climbing fast and moving with rapid wingbeats, went swinging off to the west.

"Well, I guess we did a little better on that jump shot," John said. "I always feel a little sad, but they will eat good, and there's one thing about it. If it weren't for the people who like to hunt them, there wouldn't be ducks."

"I know that," Kirk said. "I told Anne that, but she can't understand why we want to kill anything."

"I *don't* want to kill anything," John said. "All I want to do is hunt 'em."

They walked forward down the bank, and they

could see the two ducks floating thirty feet out in the water.

"Okay, Fido," John said. "Go get 'em, boy."

Kirk grinned, took off his hunting coat, put the gun on the ground, picked up a stick, and waded into the water. His feet sank deeply into the mud underneath. He struggled forward, each step stirring clouds of gray-black ooze. For a moment he unzipped his helmet and sniffed; yes, the gaseous smell of swamp mud in the cold wind was good. Good God! How he hated to be shut off from all this! He would rather be like John up there on the bank—cold, shivering a little bit, wet and thoroughly enjoying it. Smelling all the sharp smells, feeling the wind on his face, not shut off from the environment completely. The water wasn't very deep; it didn't get to Kirk's waist. He picked up one duck, a very handsome mallard drake, yellow toes curled, bright with greens and blues and the white band. He found the duller colored hen a little farther on. They were heavy and solid in his hand. He looked at them and felt sorry just as John had said he felt.

"Good boy," John said when he staggered out on the bank with a duck in each hand. "You make a fine retriever, Kirk." He looked at the ducks. "Drake and hen. I'm rather glad. We probably got a pair, they were together when they went up. One day, Gregory and I were in a beaver bog and a couple of green-winged teal flew over. Greg knocked down the female. The male flew on and made a big circle. It was just about sunset, kind of a bleak day like this. The male made a great circle half a mile across and flew around and over us again, looking down to see what had happened. We missed him, and I felt sorry about it."

There weren't too many ducks. They saw a lot of them flying; they stayed high mostly. They got one or two more shots at ducks leaping from the edge. John got a teal and they saw four wood ducks swimming close in and neither wanted to shoot.

"The prettiest birds in North America, I think," John said.

They came to a point of land, having walked first for three hundred yards through a wood of great, well-separated pine trees. This was a stopping place, and Kirk sat on the ground, his suit impervious to moisture. John sat on a stump and they leaned the guns against a nearby tree. John took a sandwich from his pocket.

"I'm sorry that you can't eat, Kirk. Right about this point a sandwich always tastes pretty good to me."

"Yes, I'm sorry too. This damn suit always keeps me away from natural things. I don't mind it most of the time, but sometimes I hate it."

"I know," John said.

They talked casually but warmly, and in this moment Kirk realized that all barriers had dropped away between them. They were just two men sitting together in the wet woods, by the marsh, the wind blowing across and ruffling the cattails and ruffling the water and flapping the edge of John's cap with an occasional strong gust. They talked of the old days, of the things that had happened then. Of those first accidents, of all of the plants that had been placed in the thinly populated, well-watered areas. They spoke of the rush for power, pushed on

160

by AEC, which had grown to the most powerful, single body in the United States, since it ruled absolutely the world of nuclear power. Power kept the world alive and killed it at the same time. Man had poisoned the natural cycle that keeps everything alive. Technology had brought them to this. Technology tried now to cure the evil. The great air plants were absolutely essential; otherwise the entire earth would by now have been covered with poisoned air. The deradders were essential. The Rs on hands for warning so that a man always could instantly tell if he were becoming dangerously subject to radiation; they spoke of these as well.

"We failed to control population," John said. "We talked about it a lot, but we went right ahead and increased in numbers. Partially this was the Catholic Church, but also partially responsible was the greed of businessmen and the demand for an ever-increasing cycle. The Gross National Product madness. Mostly it was because we simply did not control ourselves. People talked about the environment and saving the environment, but"—John took out his pipe and looked up at the sky—"when we came to doing without the slightest thing, most people simply weren't interested. Housewives demanded their detergents, phosphates or no phosphates. People shopping for beer and cold drinks refused to take the alternative of returnable bottles. The automobile owners demanded bigger, heavier, fancier automobiles. They always wanted the other man to take care of pollution. Let technology do it. Well, technology couldn't do it without the individual, and that was the philosophy that scragged us in the end, Kirk. Business as usual, the demand for more electric power, and for power over people. The self-indulgence along every line. Well, you look around you and see where it's led us."

"We don't have any population problem anymore, do we, sir?" Kirk asked.

"No, there's no population problem in Robert country. As a matter of fact our population now is less than it was fifteen years ago. However, the population in the urban centers in Normal country is immense. I know you have controlled it, you've brought it to zero population growth; but what are you going to do with all the hundreds of millions of people you have there now? All demanding power. As a matter of fact, the very maintenance of their lives demand power. Something must be done soon, Kirk."

They sat for a moment in silence. A gang of red-winged blackbirds flew over, lit on cattails and reeds bowing in the wind, shaking down their cries with the sighing of the wind in the pine trees and across the water. A flight of ducks arrowed with quickly beating wings down the center of the marsh, heading somewhere.

John said, "Blacks, black mallards. They're wise old birds. They're not about to come over here, you needn't reach for your gun."

It was a day for frankness. "Don't you people ever get mad at us Normals?" Kirk asked.

"Not the young ones like you," John Martin said slowly. "You were brought up into it. You've been trapped in your own destiny just as all the rest of us have. Trapped by our greed, our self-indulgence, by our concentration on materials, unessential luxuries, gadgets like the snowmobiles that invaded Vermont in incredible numbers, bought by people supposedly poor, and fouling up the world." He snorted. "That's what's done us in, so I don't really hold it against individuals. Some of the older ones, yes. The birds on the AEC, that incredible organization, and the Army Corps of Engineers, which has not hesitated to sacrifice the earth itself in order to keep itself in power. I resent those. I resent them because they are robbing me of the freedom to travel. They are robbing the children of Roberts everywhere of the chances for education and for training, because some of the best colleges and universities cannot or will not take them. But actually I'm not really angry even at them. I feel sorry for them."

"Why?" Kirk asked. "I'm angry at them myself sometimes, and I'm not even a Robert."

John smiled. "I think that the prejudice they feel is a result of an immense feeling of guilt. They feel guilty toward the Roberts. All you Norms subconsciously feel guilty about us, and therefore that guilt moves into fear and into dislike and into prejudice. Guilt is the worst emotion that the human spirit can endure. Guilt, there's guilt all over Normal country. Every time I go there I feel it. That's why your Normal country is so frantic. That's why it's so oversexual. You try to hide your feeling of guilt and your despair for the future in sex. Sex is fine and wonderful, but it won't solve these problems. God, I feel sorry for you young people these days. I don't think sex is nearly as much fun for your generation as it was for mine." His eyes twinkled. "Your exaggerated dress in Norm country is an instance, I think, of the agitation coming from guilt. All the hurrying, all the stomach ulcers, the heart attacks. I feel sorry for you, for the Normals."

"How about me?" Kirk asked.

"I like you," John Martin said and grinned. "Caught you in time."

"All right," Kirk said. "Thank you, sir. Now, what should be done to help things?"

"That's easy to say, but hard to do. Open the world to Roberts again. Start giving Robert children the best possible education at the best universities and the best centers of learning in Normal country. Every institution must have an area prepared so that Roberts can live there, unsuited, and learn. Let our children be powermasters, engineers, Supreme Court justices; increase our representation in the Congress. Maybe there are fewer of us than there are Normals, but we have given more. We must control the power that destroyed our country in its creation. We will sell it to the Normals, or collect a royalty. We have no intention of cutting off the supply, but many Roberts are quite poor and I think they deserve more of the better things. There should be a deradder in every home. We need each other, the Normals and the Roberts. We must not let the wall between us grow higher. Above all, above everything, we want to stop the spread of nuclear power. We want to get rid of the plants already in operation—gradually, of course, but get rid of them. Something must be done to end the polluting of our world."

"I agree, John. I can see what radiation has done to so many people, and I can also see that if we go

164

on as we are, eventually everyone will be radiated, there will be no more Normal country. But what, in the name of Heaven, can we do? Oil is gone. Coal pollutes the air and isn't available in the immense quantities needed. What can we do?"

"Develop solar power. It—"

Kirk tried hard to keep it in, the laughter bubbling and swelling up within him. He was determined not to laugh, but it burst through. He couldn't help it. He threw back his head and laughed, groping for a handkerchief. When he had dried his eyes he looked at John, expecting to see hurt anger. Instead his friend was looking at him with compassion.

"God," Martin murmured. "To think of being able to do that with a human mind." He shook his head, his face sad. "Kirk," he said quietly, "it works. I'll show you when we get home."

"Yes, sir," said Kirk, almost losing control again. "Say it works. But do you think you can make the power companies use it? They know what is best for the world."

"We'll make them do it!" Kirk was surprised at John's firm, cold tones. There was real intention there, and a knowledge of something that was beyond him.

"I hope it works, and that you can make them adopt it," he said. "I'd like to see the world restored."

"Good." For a moment Kirk thought that the older man was going on, was going to tell him something, expose a thing that lay almost exposed between them. But John's expression changed. "There's another reason why I feel sorry for the

Normals," he said, smiling again after all the seriousness.

"What is it?"

"Because I think—think, mind you—that the future belongs to us. Whoa! Here come some black ducks. Scrunch down, son, behind the bush, out of sight. They're coming our way, maybe we'll get a shot. Don't you move now, don't you move!"

Almost upon them, nearly in range, the black ducks suddenly wheeled as one and slanted off into the marshes, and Kirk heard John curse and then laugh.

Somber night had fallen before they got all the gear into John's car, and they drove home through blackness, with rain falling again. Diana welcomed them at the basement door, very much impressed by the half-dozen ducks Kirk was carrying.

"I know two brave duck hunters who will be doing some picking and cleaning tomorrow," she said.

John groaned. "I tried to give them to Kirk, but he refused. Said he wanted to taste your black duck with apples and wild rice."

Kirk dried off his suit with the large towel Diana gave him, and then followed John upstairs to where a warm fire was quietly burning in the fireplace. He took fifteen minutes and had a drink with his friend, envying the deep pleasure in John's face as he stretched stockinged feet to the blaze.

Martin put his drink on the stand and turned toward Kirk.

"There's something I've got to tell you. I'll ask you to keep it to yourself, if you will. I know it is going to be a shock to you."

"All set," said Kirk lazily, feeling the fire's warmth because of his unzipped helmet.

A shock? The laziness fell away as he did a mental double take. At first he had thought John to be joking. Now he realized the somberness that had lain beneath the words, saw the sadness in his friend's face. Kirk tensed. Something about Anne? Oh Lord! John's next two words took him wholly by surprise.

"Solar power," John said.

Had it not been so unexpected, Kirk might have fought off the laughter. As it was, he roared, choked, roared again, and then fought the laughter down, not wanting to hurt John's feelings. But John didn't look angry or hurt, only infinitely sad.

"Why do you laugh?" John asked quietly.

"Why—I don't know. It just doesn't work, you know. Everybody knows that."

"The energy cells don't work? The ones that turn the sun's rays into electricity?"

"Of course they don't, John. They taught us all about them at the University, and then again at the Power Academy. They don't last, they burn out in a few days, the power is undependable. The cells break down, the power is unreliable. Solar energy couldn't possibly furnish a hundredth of a percent of our power needs."

"But why is that funny?"

"Gosh . . . well, I guess maybe all the Econuts—the environmentalists always screaming about solar power, back in the Twentieth Century, and trying to stop nuclear power. I guess it's just—"

"Pavlovian dogs and the conditioned reflex, my friend. You have been taught, like all Normals,

167

from your earliest years, that solar power doesn't work, you have been conditioned to laugh at its mention. Pretty smart men, some time ago, who arranged that. Laughter is a very potent weapon, my boy. Ridicule. You know, Kirk, it is pitiful to watch you when solar power is mentioned—see! You smiled even when I just said the words. What a job of conditioning they did on you!"

"Oh, come now, John."

"Didn't they teach you at the Academy, drum i into you at the Academy, that solar power wouldn't work, was funny, ridiculous? Didn't they make jokes of it all the time? In your freshman year, didn't you have to ridicule, make light of, crap on, the idea of solar power all the time?"

"Well, yes."

"Didn't you *ever* wonder why?"

"I guess we were too busy to do much wondering."

"Didn't they sleep-teach you a lot? Put small speakers under your pillow and drill you as you slept? Of course they did."

"Sure. We used that technique. It helped a lot in memorizing some of the things we had to know."

"But you don't really know what you were taught, do you."

"I thought I did."

"Certainly." John sighed. "Kirk, we had sunshine all day yesterday. Now, the lights you are sitting by, the oil furnace circulator pump, the electric stove in the kitchen, all of these are at this minute being powered by solar power. *Don't laugh!*"

Kirk controlled himself. He didn't feel like

laughing. Poor John! Where did he get this delusion?

"I have the power cells on the roof," John said. "I have twelve batteries in the basement, with a converter for changing the DC to AC, at the needed voltage and cycles. I'm also hooked into VPC lines. Here in Vermont, with antiquated equipment, you can't depend wholly on solar power. But even in the darkest time of the year, it helps. I ask you to keep this quiet. VPC would refuse to give me any power if they knew that I had a solar outfit here. They've been pulling that for years."

Kirk sat, at first not much affected, then as thought went through layer after layer, deeper into blackness, he began to reel with the implications. Could he believe John? Could he disbelieve this man? He could not. Then why . . . ?

"You mustn't just accept my word," John said. "We'll go down and check the batteries. Come up tomorrow and I'll take you on the roof—you can see them in operation if the sun is shining, or if the clouds aren't too thick."

"But John it won't last long. They don't stand up. Why, we—"

"They have been in operation for thirty years," John said calmly.

"My God!" Cardboard castles, the base pulled out, began to crumble, the entire edifice to sway. "Who invented the system? Where did you get it?"

"It was invented for use in the Apollo Program, for spacecraft, back in the 1960s. In the 1970s they discovered how to make the energy cells in mass production, so that they could have been made as cheap as transistors within a few years. But it was never done. The power companies blocked it. They ridiculed it. They controlled Congress and the entire government. They killed solar energy."

"Why?"

"Kirk, if every house, every factory, had a solar power system, as could be made perfectly practical, where would the power companies be? They couldn't figure out a way to monopolize the sun. So they killed solar energy. They had billions and billions of dollars invested in nuclear energy. Through controlled politicians they could milk the government of many billions more. It is the old viciousness, Kirk. All power corrupts; absolute power corrupts absolutely. The power companies had tremendous power over the human race; they wanted to keep it. They kept it. They have ended by being totally corrupted, supported and protected by their own creatures, the Atomic Energy Commission and the Nuclear Regulatory Commission."

"We've saved the world!" Kirk cried. "Deny that?"

"You've ruined the world!" John snapped. "Now you are keeping it alive—for a time. But if you go on as you are, you will totally destroy it. You know that, when you let yourself think. It is a holding action alone."

Kirk sat stunned. The minute minder in his helmet whirred. Budget time expired. He zipped up, closing himself off from the radiated air, from his friend's close presence.

"I'd better go, I guess," he said. "Get some sleep before my watch." He was remembering Sneck.

170

"That goddamn Martin has too low a power bill. Gotta watch him."

John stood up, his face bleak.

"Where did you get the cells?" Kirk asked, trying to recreate doubt.

"A couple of factories in Robert country make them. Jury-rigged. The same old 1970 designs. No research possible with our facilities. A lot of people you know here are using them. Gregory is. Won't use anything else. When the sun doesn't shine, he uses wood for heat and lamps for light. Ask him."

"Thanks a lot, John," Kirk said, recalling manners. "I'd better go."

"Are you going to turn me in, Kirk?" John looked him squarely in the eyes through the clear plastic of the helmet.

"Christ, no, John!" Kirk cried. He put his suited arm around John's shoulders. "You know I won't. I'd never do anything to hurt you, or my other friends here. And when I get to be anything but a second-class messenger boy in VPC, I'm going to damn well see that we develop solar power!"

"You smiled when you said the words, Kirk."

"Can't get rid of the training that quick, John. But I'll make people quit laughing at it. Good-bye, John. I've got to go think. God, how I've got to think!"

He almost forgot the whole thing as he was driving south; for a time it almost seemed as if nothing had happened to him, as if the conversation had been the merest trifle between gossiping friends. He thought of Dead Creek and ducks, and most of all of Anne. Passing into the dome from the black and rainy night was like a transition into another world. No rain fell there. The interior was softly lighted, as if by moonlight, and from the windows of quarters and wardroom bright lights shone out. The air was at exactly the right temperature and humidity; somebody was swimming in the pool. Outside in the woods and on the lake rain was falling, beginning to freeze into sleet now, a sharp wind was blowing, and everything was wet and black with cold. In here—warmth, light from homes, comfort, comradeship. It was, in a sense, like awakening from a nightmare to find the old reliable world about one.

Kirk felt something close to fear as he looked around the dome. Was this vanishing? Was it part of a gigantic structure built on lies? The utter physical comfort of this enclosed world sank over him. Outside it rained, sleeted. Inside it could also rain. The control computer picked randomly a few two-hour periods each week during which a gentle, soaking rain fell inside the dome. It was necessary for the vegetation. It was also necessary for the people psychologically. At first the rain had been publicly scheduled in advance, but it had been found that an element of uncertainty was needed. A man might curse if the rain began while he was playing tennis, for instance, but that was a healthy frustration. "I hope it won't rain" hadn't fallen into disuse in the language of the Normals working in the power domes.

Kirk pushed his doubts and the weight of foreboding aside, cleaned up in his room, and went to the wardroom for dinner. Married officers whose wives were present had cooking facilities in their quarters, but most of them chose to dine in the wardroom. Drinks preceded the meal, and Kirk took three martinis tonight, feeling that he needed them. They always made him sleepy after the meal, and he felt that he would need help to get to sleep tonight, when he was alone in the dark, and the lurking presence John had invoked could no longer be kept out of his mind. This time it didn't work. He had a hard time getting to sleep.

Could he believe John? No matter how he squirmed mentally, he came up with the conviction that he could. Martin would not lie to him. That Martin had been lied to, was himself deceived, offered some hope. But how? He would, on the next sunny day, check those cells. He had seen some of them in the Academy museum in a section entitled "Jokes." They had been there along with models of windmills, methane gas converters, perpetual-motion machines, a machine that had been designed to convert water to gasoline, and some amazing, many-angled and cogwheeled Rube Goldbergs that made a powerman laugh. But he remembered vaguely what they looked like, and he remembered strongly his incredulity that men once had hoped that such gadgets could ever replace the giant nukes that were going to be his entire life. He could check the cells. But how could he check as to how long they had been in operation? He would have to rely on John. Maybe John had preserved his power bills; Kirk could easily tell whether or not he had had an auxiliary power supply. VPC would have the records, but if Sneck was already suspicious, he wouldn't want to bring further attention upon John. It was not illegal to do what John had said he was doing, but the power company could shut off its power entirely, and in the cold, dark winter ahead that would be a miserable thing for John and his family, even if the solar energy did work.

Put that aside. Say that solar energy did work. Say that John had lived in comfort for thirty years with his own solar power supply. What then?

Why then, then . . . the whole structure was false. If a small outmoded unit, hand made, could supply a house, then power technology could create units that could, with long-range transmission, replace much of the nuclear power. It could certainly obviate the necessity of building ever more plants, with ever more radiation, and ever more radioactive waste. Kirk knew that even the ocean itself was growing dirty. There was no more ocean swimming for Normals, and all seafood had to be deradded, wherever caught. The day was inevitably coming when all of the oceans of the world would be lethally radioactive. Ocean life had mutated during the gradual change; many species had died out, others had changed. Kirk remembered a lecture given by an oceanographer and marine biologist. Whales still survived in small numbers, not enough to hunt. Porpoises had grown larger and less numerous. They no longer played around the bows of vessels; instead they fled at the sound of a propeller. Swimmers had been attacked by porpoises, some killed. Kirk seemed to remember that the porpoise had, before radiation, been strangely friendly to man, had even rescued swimmers in distress, had played with children on beaches. Porpoises had nearly been wiped out by the tuna fishermen, drowning them purposely in their great nets by the hundred thousand every year. When the tuna fish had been destroyed, that fishing ceased, but the porpoises were by then totally avoiding man. Marineland had had to enclose its tanks with steel netting because so many spectators had been injured by leaping, slashing porpoises. Kirk thought of the wolverdeer and shuddered.

Well, solar power could end all that—at least the growing change. Perhaps the damage already done could not be reversed, but it need not be increased. Damn it all, the power industry *could* adopt solar energy for the needs of the world—if John's setup had indeed lasted for thirty years. It would at least help! Kirk's head whirled with the possibilities that he could see. Square miles of cells in the Southwest! John's setup, he had said, covered twelve square feet, and in sunny weather gave him enough amperage at 110 volts and 60 cycles to entirely run a house. And that was with antiquated equipment. Efficiency could certainly be increased. Kirk had always known that the sun was a tremendous, eternal hydrogen bomb exploding forever, a nuclear plant in the sky, bathing the earth's surface with enough energy to dwarf all the present or foreseeable needs of man. If man were only able to put it to work . . . And, apparently, man could.

But the whole mighty structure, the power complex that ruled and saved the world, it was built on a lie. Maybe a mistake, an honest one, but still Kirk could not forget the years of conditioning that he had undergone, the constant denigration of solar power. And yet that in itself should prove something. A man or an institution did not con-

175

stantly attack *anything* of which it was not, somewhere inside, afraid.

Then what of Kirk's career? He had thought of himself as one of the trained saviors of the world, technologically speaking. Now what? Was he instead the trained and devoted supporter of a system based on greed, power lust, ignorance? A system that would rule the world even if it ruined it in the process? This was something he was going to have to decide. And soon.

It was late when he went to sleep; he had barely an hour of oblivion when he was called for his watch. He felt groggy and uneasy, unsure of himself, but when that key was in the board and he was seated before it, all the old sureness, the alertness, the sense of power and command came back, and it was again as if he had awakened from a nightmare.

Chapter Eight /

THE HEARING

On days when Kirk had no plans he slept through
lunch and awakened in the early afternoon. One
day he thus came awake at about two o'clock with
someone knocking at his door.

"Come in."

Carl Dundee, a young technician at the plant,
thrust his head through the door, said, "Hi, Kirk.
The boss would like to see you."

"Oh." Kirk rubbed the sleep out of his eyes.
"When?"

"Right away. Soon as you can make it."

"Okay. I wonder what the flap is."

"I don't know. Something from New York.
Maybe they're going to make you supervisor, old
boy."

"Sure, that's it," Kirk said, climbing out of bed.
He'd gotten reasonably accustomed to the night
shift, and after he'd showered and dressed he felt
alert and rested. He walked out of the bachelor officers' quarters and across the summer yard, for
within the dome an even temperature was
maintained. The air was cool and invigorating, yet
warm enough for shirtsleeves.

George Sneck's secretary smiled at him when he

arrived at the office. "He's waiting for you. Go ahead in." Sneck's rather round, bland face was inscrutable this time, as Kirk came into the room.

"You wanted to see me, sir?"

"Yes, Kirk. Sit down."

Kirk sat. Sneck swiveled his chair, looked up at the portrait of Meredith on the wall, then out of the window and across the domed yard at the woodland and the mountains that lay beyond, with snow on their peaks.

"Well, Patrick," he said, "I talked to you some time ago, remember?"

"Yes, sir."

"I told you that the company didn't like too much fraternization. They feel it's kind of unhealthy. I tried to give you the best kind of advice I could give. Right?"

"I suppose so." Kirk began to wonder what was coming; he knew what it was connected with now. Sneck had been less and less friendly since their previous encounter.

"Your work here," Sneck said, "has been all right. You're a competent powerman, no doubt about it, but you haven't added much to the life and gaiety in this plant. You haven't been here that much."

"I didn't think that was required, sir."

"Of course it's not required, not in writing, not officially, but all the same you're expected to be part of the family and you haven't been, you've been gone all the time. And it's not bad enough to be done, but you're also with Roberts. Grouse hunting, deer hunting, courting. My God, courting!"

178

"Sir," Kirk said, "I think my personal affairs can stay out of this."

"All right, you just tell the board that."

"What board, sir?"

Sneck was shuffling some papers. "Here are your orders. This is the fifteenth. Day after tomorrow, the seventeenth, you are to report at ten-thirty in the morning to VPC headquarters, New York, for the hearing as prescribed by company rules."

"Hearing?"

"That's right, you're going down for an evaluation hearing. The board will decide whether to fire you, transfer you to some other station, or return you to duty here at V7. Sorry, Patrick, but I warned you."

"I will be damned!" Kirk said.

Sneck shook his head. "Yeah, I know, maybe it doesn't seem right to you, but you see, what's all right for anybody else isn't all right for a powerman. We're too important."

Kirk felt a little dazed. The coming year had stretched ahead in bright prismatic gaiety in his mind. There would be Anne, the intolerable frustration of seeing her and loving her and never being able to speak of it or hold her or touch her, but there would be Anne. And there would be the lovely world about him, and the friends, and skiing in the winter and fishing in the spring and hiking the mountains in the summer. It was to have been a happy and fulfilling year.

"Okay," he said. "Is that it?" Goddamn bastards! he thought, clinching teeth to keep the words in, clinching fists for battering Sneck's round face.

"Yep, that's all."

179

Kirk decided to go into town and see Anne and John and any of the others he might happen to encounter. He thought he might as well tell them it was very possible that his period at Waybury was coming to a rather abrupt close. Gregory and Liz were at John's house, and it rather touched Kirk to see the absolute dismay that his announcement caused. Gregory dropped his pipe, reached over and fumbled for it.

"Goddamn," he said. "Get a good man here and they go drag him back."

John looked shocked and grieved.

"What for, Kirk?" he asked. "Why are they sending you back?"

"Well, of course, I think the board will return me to duty all right," Kirk said, pleased at the consternation his news had caused. "They say that I . . . I . . ."

"Yeah, you've been seeing too much of us Roberts," Gregory growled.

"Yes, I guess that's it."

John shook his head and a slow, rueful smile came over his face. "Well, Kirk, I sure hope they send you back up. We'll miss you if they don't. You see what I mean, don't you, about the wall that's growing higher and higher and that I think endangers our country more than even the radiation? Good luck to you, boy, and I hope it works out."

Diana and Liz both seemed extremely grieved by the news of Kirk's difficulties. All four sat with him on the carport and helped him curse the company and the rules and the stupidity that would allow the power structure to behave in such a fashion.

John said, "It's guilt, of course, Kirk. You remember we talked about that out at Dead Creek. I think that they're afraid of us, but I don't think that they have any reason to be. There is no difference between us, really. The Roberts don't want to tear down the country or upset the structure, or ruin the rest of the world, any more than the Norms want us to, but they feel guilty and afraid, and it's one of the old tragic facts of mankind that guilt and fear soon turn to hate."

"Fuck 'em!" Gregory growled. "Give them the old sweet talk, boy. Tell them you were just doing a psychological study of the Robert makeup, mentality, and reactions. Tell them you were going in for an advanced degree in power study. Tell them that this was just a test case, that you were doing a random sample of the Robert population. Tell them how nutty John here is. Tell them we're all scared to death of the Norms. Anxious to do anything they want us to and perfectly willing to go on living in poverty in Robert country. Tell them anything they'd like to hear."

"Okay," Kirk said, "I'll do it."

Telling Anne was hard. He called on her at her apartment. The small living room was bright and cheerful, with pictures on the wall and books everywhere.

"What's the matter, Kirk?" she asked. "You look worried. Even behind that windshield you look worried."

"I guess I am, Anne," he said. He told her.

For a moment he thought she was going to cry. Then she shook her head and smiled at him, though the tears were still sparkling in her eyes, and said, "That's what you get for associating with us Scarlet Women."

"Oh, Anne!"

"The scarlet letter . . . the orange letter . . . the *fluorescent orange letter* . . ." she said a little bitterly. "Hawthorne should have written it. I wonder if anyone ever *will* write it?"

He stepped close to her and she pulled back a little and said, "No, no, I might contaminate you, you might catch my orange letter."

"If you talk that way, I'll take this suit off and never put it back on again."

"Oh, Kirk," she said, "don't be an idiot!"

She left the room a moment, and when she came back she was smiling and apparently relaxed. He didn't stay there long. He never did. Perhaps temptation was too much.

The seventeenth was gray and there were a few flurries of snow in the air. Kirk had been excused from his tour on the board the night before, and he got up while night was still dark outside the dome. His plane left Burlington at eight o'clock. He breakfasted, feeling a little sickness from suspense. He got ready and folded his suit carrier; he carried only it and a briefcase. Strange to think that soon he would be outdoors without a suit on.

"Good luck!" Frank Owen said, shaking his hand. He and Carl Dundee were waiting by the air lock gate through which Kirk was to drive his car. Carl also held out his hand. "Good luck, Kirk. I think it stinks. Tell 'em so, but come on back."

Mary Owen was there too. She kissed Kirk on the cheek and squeezed his gloved hand. He rolled up the window, sealed the car, and drove away.

The jets hadn't changed very much. They were a little faster, very much quieter, very, very much cleaner. Theirs and the military aircraft's were virtually the only combustion engines allowed to operate, and controls were rigid on them. Soft music was playing as Kirk came aboard. The stewardess checked his ticket and smiled mechanically at him as he went up the carpeted aisle. People were surging onto the plane, everyone suited. A third of them had their helmets open, and he knew them to be Roberts. He found a seat by one of the small oval windows and squirmed himself into comfort in it. He put his briefcase and suitbag beneath the seat in front of him and fastened the strap. He looked out. A few people were still coming across the concrete apron to board.

"Good morning. Welcome aboard Mohawk Airlines Flight 343, Burlington, Vermont, to Kennedy Airport, New York. If you are not familiar with the plane, please read the card of instructions in the seat pocket before you. We hope you enjoy your flight. Your captain is Hiram Bosworth, your stewardess, Jane Adler. Welcome aboard."

The motors were started. They screamed, then muted down to a whisper. The plane vibrated. The public address system clicked and the stewardess's pleasant, well-modulated voice said, "We are about to seal, we are about to seal. Will all Roberts please seal suits. Seal suits, please."

An awkward feeling swept through the plane. At least it seemed awkward to Kirk. No one said anything. The twenty or so Roberts aboard zipped shut their helmets and pressed the sealing buttons,

183

placing power packs and air-circulation systems in operation.

"Thank you. The plane is now sealing."

The red light came on beneath the No Smoking sign in the forward end of the passenger compartment. Air sighed, then in a moment the light went off.

"We are now sealed. Thank you. I hope you all enjoy the flight. A stewardess will be circulating with coffee, Danish pastry, and juice very shortly. No smoking. Please observe the lighted sign."

Kirk unzipped his helmet. In a moment the plane took off. A hundred yards from the ground it ran into the grayness of low haze, surged through it for a minute or two, then emerged into bright sunlight at several thousand feet. Kirk settled back for the flight, uneasy about the ordeal that lay ahead but hopeful that everything would be all right.

The plane flew on course for thirty minutes, circled Kennedy for thirty minutes, and landed. Getting from the plane to the terminal took another ten, but Kirk still had plenty of time. Once in the terminal, where there was room to swing his arms, he stepped aside and removed his protective suit. He folded it expertly, zipped it into his carrying pack, and, carrying suit pack in one hand and briefcase in the other, walked off through the terminal, heading for the monorail station. Already he had begun to feel strange palpitations in his blood, a kind of a pressure from all sides, a feeling of mental unease and contagion arising from a mass of people all around him. The monorail was crowded at this time of the morning. He couldn't get a seat, so he stood holding to a strap as the train hurtled along in its single track, silent except for the scream and rush of air. People were packed hip to hip, shoulder to shoulder, back to front all about him. Those seated looked trapped behind their newspapers. Those standing looked caught up in misery. He got out at Grand Central and carried himself through the surging maelstrom of rushing people bouncing off one another. He saw the marquees of theaters. It felt very, very strange to be out in the open air without a suit. That he liked; he breathed deeply. The air here was clean. It didn't have the freshness of the forest air of Vermont on those few occasions on which he had opened his helmet for budget time, but it was clean. The skyscrapers stood out sharply and the sky was blue. There was no doubt that the conversion to atomic power had been immensely beneficial in many ways to society. The old loyalties began to surge back as he looked at the transformation that had taken place in this once-grimy city.

The Empire State Building, pushing its way up among its taller neighbors, had a solid, old-fashioned look about it as he approached it. It seemed like coming home. The first stop after the outer receptionist was the medical office. The medical examination was extremely searching this time, with particular attention being paid to any vestiges of radiation or any chemical changes caused by radiation. Some suspense arose in Kirk's mind as the procedure went through its complex yet swiftly moving steps. The testing machines, the quick blood samples, urine samples, all the rest of the samples, the waiting for ten minutes trying to relax, and then the doctor's report.

"You're clean, Mr. Patrick. I would say that you've been quite careful during your stay in Robert country. I will send this along to the board, of course."

The receptionist outside the boardroom, a beautiful redheaded girl, was wearing one of the new see-through dress tops. It made her look as if she were nude from the waist up, misted with dark blue shadow. She was using bright bronze, rather metallic-looking nipplesticks that looked a little hard to Kirk. He liked the see-through tops, though he thought that the wrong people sometimes wore them. He took his mind from the receptionist and looked at the racked magazines. He found a copy of *Vermont Life*, picked it up, and began to look through the colorful photographs. His hands were sweating and he was having trouble getting air enough into his lungs. Even through the walls and the big windows, there came always from below and all around the distant, dull, pulsing roar of the city. It had quieted much over the years, he was told; but still, the mere presence of those millions of people made a wall of sound one's ear heard without hearing it, and always there was the surf-like background sound of the air plants. In a little while the intercom on the desk buzzed gently. The girl spoke into it.

"You can go in now, Mr. Patrick."

She opened the door for him, and then closed it with her on the outside. Kirk missed her; she was a nice sight.

It was a boardroom, carpeted, draped, with large

windows and a massive table. The seven or eight men sitting around the other end of the table were executives. He saw the Powermaster of Vermont, who was looking at him like someone observing an insect. At the head of the table was Mr. Steve Bright, the VPC Powermaster. Kirk's stomach turned over a little bit. This must be serious, to get the top brass in like that, as well as personnel vice-presidents, morale officers, and public relations people. Mr. Bright took casual, easy charge.

"Good morning, Mr. Patrick. It was good of you to come down to see us. Will you sit down, please, at the end of the table?"

Kirk sat down behind an ashtray and a glass of water. The chair was comfortable, padded and molded to fit the body, but it felt like sitting on a rack. He was sweating.

"Mr. Patrick," said Steve Bright, "you are down here to face certain charges. Charges is perhaps too strong a word, but the Powermaster of Vermont has insisted that they may be serious."

"Yes, sir," Kirk said.

"Your supervisor says that your work has been good. We have no complaints there, I'm glad to say, and that, as far as I'm concerned, is most important, but he feels that you spend a very excessive amount of time in the company of Roberts, male and female. Is that true?"

"No, sir," Kirk said.

The Powermaster of Vermont sat up straight and started to glare at him.

"I spend a lot of time with Roberts. I have come to know and like them, and I don't think it's excessive time."

Bright consulted the report. "There is a Robert young lady whom you see quite often."

"Yes sir, there certainly is, and I think that is my business."

"Well, young man, it's your business to a certain extent, but it is also the company's business. We demand that our people stay—I don't like the word—but stay clean, not irradiated. You don't want to look down at your hand and see that fluorescent R there one day, do you?"

"No, sir. I'm careful, I take only budget time."

"Your medical report confirms that, Mr. Patrick, but you haven't been there very long."

A new voice spoke up, that of a gray-headed man with a bristly moustache. "Mr. Patrick, since you see a good deal of the Roberts, do you find any feeling of dislike or unease in the area? Is there any suggestion of—what should I call it—dissatisfaction with the power companies? With things as they presently are?"

"Yes, sir," Kirk answered.

"Explain that, please. With what are they dissatisfied?"

"That's easy, sir, and I must say that I generally agree with them. They don't like the constant spread of nuclear plants in their country, placed wherever the power companies want and when they want, with the Roberts having no say in the matter."

"Nonsense," growled a third man. "Don't the fools know what is good for them?"

"They see the increasing radiation, sir, and the increasing numbers of deformed children, and the growing cancer rate."

"Bah! Without nuclear power they couldn't even stay alive."

"Neither could we, sir. Without the nuclear plants in Robert country, Normal country would not be Normal long. How long would it take to wipe us out? Six months? A year?"

"Goddamn it, sir! What are you suggesting?"

"Nothing, sir, except to say that the obligation runs both ways. I have found absolutely nothing among the Roberts to indicate that they have any thought whatever of shutting off the power to us Normals. They know it is a two-way road. All of us need it."

"Hmph. I think you're a troublemaker, Patrick. Maybe even a goddamn conservationist!"

"Gentlemen! Mr. Loris! I must ask that you cease using offensive language. Mr. Patrick is one of our officers, an expert and very capable man. He is devoted to the company. I will not have you calling him a conservationist, sir. Every man is innocent until he is proven guilty."

"Very nice to say, Bright, but self-preservation is another matter. What else do the Roberts want?"

"Royalties on the power." A gasp went up, followed by muttered conversation. "Free travel. Robertized buildings in all colleges and universities. More places in Congress, in the courts, and in the power companies."

"Good God!"

"It seems reasonable to me." Kirk smiled. "I think they even want us to try to develop solar power." He laughed, deprecatingly. He expected the usual roar of laughter, but there was none.

"So. It is worse than I thought. Bright, I think we've heard enough. I'm ready for a vote."

"I second that motion." The grunter of this remark was the Powermaster, Vermont. He was looking at Kirk as if he had a filthy taste in his mouth. Other voices spoke, other heads nodded. Bright looked faintly regretful.

"Very well, Mr. Patrick. Will you wait outside for a few moments? We will call you back shortly."

Kirk hardly even looked at the receptionist's breasts as he went out of the room. He was thinking of the Green Mountains, scarlet and gold in the fall, of his friends, of the gray, silver, and brown of the duck marsh. He was thinking of John and Gregory, the cheerful self-reliance of these people, and the uncrowded tempo of life. Most of all he was thinking of Anne. Within the next few minutes he might be told that he would never see her again. It could be orders to the Antarctic, or Greenland; he could even be remanded to a General Board for firing. In which case what could he do in Robert country? Even his suits belonged to the company, and he couldn't go north without a suit.

Within the boardroom, Bright was frowning as he returned to his seat. Loris, the gray-moustached, bristling man, was still bristling. "Christ," he said. "Do we even need to vote? He's not only fraternizing, he's also getting sympathetic to the Roberts. And solar power, by God! You know what I think? I think he's a conservationist and I think he is, potentially at any rate, a solar power man."

"Now, Richard," another man said. "I don't think he's that bad—but I must agree that I'm not at all sure he should be in so sensitive a position."

"I say fire him!" exclaimed the Powermaster, Vermont. "Damned if I want him at one of my boards. I know the type. Seen them before. This is only the beginning. First thing you know he'll be *demanding* that we develop solar energy. Fire him."

"Second the motion," said Loris.

Raymond Swift amended the motion to one to transfer Patrick to an uninhabited area, or perhaps an ocean station, or one of the polar plants. The amendment carried.

"Question," said Loris. "We've talked enough."

Swift and one other man voted against. Bright, as chairman, voted only in the case of a tie. The motion carried.

"Call him back, Steve. I want to see his face when we tell him he's bound for the icy shores of Greenland."

"One moment, gentlemen. Under our rules and company procedure, I have the power to overrule such a vote if I see fit. I do see fit. I herewith overrule you. Kirk Patrick is going to be returned to Vermont on full duty status."

The reaction was instantaneous. Loris threw his cigar into an ashtray, cursing. The Powermaster, Vermont growled something. Others muttered.

"I'll give you my thinking, gentlemen," Bright said. "Patrick has become closer to the Roberts in his area than any man we have had there in twenty years. I've had other reports than George Sneck's, you understand. Among his friends are several who are suspected of being a part of an antipower plot. We don't know what they're up to, but we've heard rumors. And—I hate to say it—

there is a good deal of solar power sentiment in all Robert country—"

"Tell us something new, Bright," growled Loris.

"All right, Raymond, I will. We have indications that a number of backyard factories in Robert country are making power cells, along the line of the old primitive 1970 Apollo models, the silicone process. Nothing big yet, just that there are indications here and there of people cutting down on power consumption from us without cutting down on use."

"Cut 'em off, goddamn it!" growled Loris. "We've got precedent enough for that. Let 'em freeze and go blind."

"It's not quite that simple. You must remember, Raymond, Patrick said that although the Roberts are wholly dependent on us for power—or were wholly dependent—and are wholly so for the anti-radiation shots—we are at the same time dependent on *them*—"

"That's a hell of a thing to say. Dependent on goddamn Roberts!"

"Our plants are in Robert country, except for the seaborne and polar plants, and they wouldn't carry the load. The Roberts *could*, if they were desperate enough, shut down the plants. Cut the lines. How long would we last? After the air plants and the deradders stopped?"

"Longer than they would without the shots."

"But suppose they learned to produce them? Don't underestimate the Roberts, gentlemen. They are as smart as we. They just don't have the physical facilities."

"Get to it, Steve. What's your idea?"

192

"That we send young Patrick back without strings. Encourage him to see as much of the Roberts as possible. I think he's a loyal sensitive young man. His sympathies are with the Roberts in some ways, but he is a powerman, with parents and family in Normal country. I am going to encourage him to continue with the Roberts, and ask him to be on the lookout for two things—the location of and method of operation of the solar-cell factories, and for *any* indication that the Roberts have learned to produce antiradiation shots."

"Do you think he would tell you about it?"

"Perhaps not, voluntarily. But certainly otherwise. We'll call him back every three months for a physical—for he is seeing a lot of the Roberts. Give him another hour's budget time. We'll want to measure the effects. Then, while he is hooked into the machines, the doctor will give him the right drugs, put him under induced hypnosis, and check his reactions to pertinent questions; he can get the information we want without Patrick even knowing that he has given it."

"Hmm. Well. Maybe you have something there. But will it work? Are you sure he won't know about it?"

Bright smiled. "Fairly sure. You see, we've already done it—this morning. It worked. He didn't even know he had been asleep and had talked. The doctor is positive. Patrick knows nothing of the location of solar cell plants, though he does know that at least one Robert is using them, and he knows absolutely nothing about shot substitutes. And he knows nothing of any concerted Robert action."

"You're clever, Steve," Loris said, stroking his little moustache and smiling grimly. "Okay, let's send the young fool back, with our blessing."

"So moved," another board member said, grinning. The motion was carried unanimously.

It seemed to Patrick that he had been lost in somber thoughts and considerable fear for a very long time when the door opened and the Vermont Powermaster stepped through.

"Mr. Patrick, we're ready for you."

Kirk went in and stood at his end of the table as the Vermont Powermaster returned to his seat. Kirk could feel his legs trembling slightly, and his breath was hard to control. Bright looked at him and smiled.

"Mr. Patrick, you are being returned to duty without prejudice."

Relief flowed over Kirk. His knees stiffened and the breath left him in a long sigh of relief. A little mutter went around the room. Kirk sneezed and breathed deeply, overflowing with pleasure now.

"Thank you, sir."

"You are not going back on any form of probation, Mr. Patrick. The board and I feel that your connections with the Roberts are of utmost diplomatic value to the company, and we all wish you to continue as you have in the past. Of course," he said, soberly, "the usual precautions concerning your health remain valid and required. With one exception. After consultation with the examining doctors this morning, we have decided that you may hereafter take two hours of budget time a week."

Wow! Kirk lit up inside. Two hours face to face with Anne! The prospect was dazzling.

"But don't overdo it." Bright was smiling again. "Moreover, as a result of this extra budget time, we want you to come down to New York every three months for a full physical. If any bad results begin to show, you will be returned at once to the old schedule."

"That's fine with me, sir."

"Good. Young man, I'd like a word with you alone. All right, gentlemen. We stand adjourned."

The board members were getting up from the table. Several shook hands with Kirk, including even, to his surprise, the smallish man with the bristly moustache and the Vermont Powermaster. Mr. Loris seemed particularly friendly, and beamed at Kirk as they shook hands. Then Kirk was alone with Bright.

"Sit down and be comfortable, Patrick. Do you smoke? Oh, a pipe. Light up, then, if you like. There's nothing to add to the official verdict of the board. I merely wanted to tell you one or two things."

"Yes, sir."

"I'm a Waybury College graduate. Did you know that?"

"No, sir!" Kirk was somehow surprised.

"Your friend, Professor Martin, was one of my professors. We used to argue a lot, but I rather liked him. I still remember some of the things he had to say. Believe it or not, I was a campus radical in those days, and I thought he was a moss-backed conservative. I guess we have rather changed places, but I have a notion he has stayed right where he was all along, while *I* changed."

"He's a very good man, sir."

"Yes, yes, he is. Others too." Bright got up and paced back and forth. "I deeply regret the separation of Normals and Roberts. I know that it is necessary as a medical precaution, but it is turning into a social barrier as well. That is why I was pleased, rather than otherwise, to find that you were coming to know many of the Roberts well. Do you really feel that they have no desire to upset the situation between us in any drastic way? Beyond the wants—and very reasonable ones they were, I'd say—that you enumerated?"

"Absolutely not, sir."

"I'm very glad. Now, we understand that there is some minor experimentation with solar power . . ." Bright smiled, and Kirk controlled a beginning laugh and smiled in reply. "Rather pitiful, of course, but understandable. Now, if you find they have discovered anything new that might be of help to us, get all the details. I would be delighted to find a process that would let us cut down on new plants."

"So would I, sir!" Kirk's eyes were shining. Wait until John and the others heard this.

"So keep your ears open for solar power. And there are brilliant Roberts—they may find something very important. Also, their medical men are working constantly on radiation sickness and its control. So find out all you can along those lines. I certainly don't want to waste the immense store of talent that lies in Robert country—disadvantaged, perhaps, but always capable of some new discovery. Now, young man, I don't mean spying. I mean information. And you need feel no obligation to tell us a thing unless you think it is wholly consistent with your loyalties to your Robert friends."

"That's wonderful, sir. You give me hope, sir."

"Good, Mr. Patrick, good. I have great confidence in you in your post in the field, on the firing line, so to speak. Do tell John Martin that I remember him warmly, and if I can do him a favor at any time I am at his command."

"I certainly will." They shook hands warmly, and when Kirk went out it was like walking on air rather than carpet. The bronze-tipped beauties of the red-haired girl swung with more joyful abandon as she walked with him across the reception room.

"Where's the nearest pay phone?" he asked. "I want to make a call." He was very anxious to hear Anne's voice again.

Chapter Nine /

SPEAK FOR YOURSELF

As Kirk drove down Route 7 to Waybury from the Burlington airport, he was feeling like someone coming home; he realized that the feeling was rooted not at the power plant but at the house on the side of the hill where John and Diana Martin lived, and especially in Anne's presence. Returned to duty without prejudice. George Sneck probably would be mad as hell, but that wouldn't lose Kirk any sleep. He stopped by John's house on the way and was touched by the reception he received. John seemed especially relieved.

Diana said, "I wish we could ask you for dinner. I've told John again and again that we must have a room somewhere in the house where we can entertain Normals. It seems so very awkward not being able to offer a friend a meal."

"It's pleasure enough to be here with you and John. Where is Anne?"

"She's down at her apartment, I'm sure," Diana said. "Do stop by and see her. She was thrilled at your call."

"That's right," John agreed. "They must have better sense down there than I thought they had. It gives me considerable hope."

Anne had cried and then laughed when Kirk gave her the news of his return over the phone. When he found her at her apartment, she was her usual, sunny self, unaffectedly glad to see him.

"I'm so pleased that you're going to be around for a while," she said, holding both his gloved hands in hers. "I should be coy, I guess, and not say it, but you do know that I'm glad."

"I don't know why you should be, dear, but I certainly am happy about it."

"While I was waiting to hear from you, I started thinking that maybe it would be best if you had to go away."

"Anne!"

"Don't look like that. You know what I mean. Anyway, as soon as I heard your voice on the phone, heard how happy you sounded, then I knew that had been nonsense and I was happy, too. I still am. Have you any budget time available?"

"I certainly do. I can take a whole half hour!"

"Then how about a cup of tea? I keep bottled, clean water, you know."

"I'd love tea, Anne, and I don't really care whether its clean or not."

"Don't be a dope; of course you care. Sit quiet; you must be tired from the trip. I'll have tea in a minute."

He sat there, listening to her humming and clattering in the kitchen, and he knew that this was why he had felt that he was coming home.

He was received warmly at the plant. Even George Sneck shook hands with him and said, "I'm glad you're back. You understand I had to make the report. It's part of my job." He glowered at Kirk, obviously hard put to restrain himself.

"Yes, George," Kirk said.

A couple of afternoons later the Martins gave a small party in honor of Kirk's happy return. The guests included those Roberts whom Kirk had already met here, the Mainyards, Ronald and Mrs. Trout, the Forrests, the Morgans, with Jim Mann and Joe Ball and their wives. Anne was present and she seemed very happy. They were all extremely interested in Steve Bright.

"I remember him," John Martin said. "He graduated about twenty years ago. A very bright young man, if you'll pardon the pun. He was also the campus radical and editor of the newspaper. Oh boy! Was he mad at the establishment! And now he's Powermaster, Vermont Power Corporation?"

"Yes, sir."

"And he said that he doesn't want the wall to get any higher?"

"Yes, he did, and he seemed very concerned."

"Maybe they're beginning to get some sense, Gregory," John said.

"Could be, but I doubt it. Steve Bright. Who'd ever think he'd learn anything in only twenty years?"

Joe Ball said, "I like his reaction to Kirk's suggestion of power royalties. I think it's too much to expect that the power companies would actually turn over the plants to us."

"We'll take 'em if they don't," Gregory said.

"Well, it's easily said, but they do require a lot of technical attention and supervision, and a lot of capital. But if the state could get royalties on the power a good many problems would be solved. It would put up the cost of power, but I think that's the lesser of a good many evils."

"Hmmmmm, yes," John said. "I've thought about royalties a good deal. We could certainly take care of all our people with a ten percent royalty charge. It would do away with the poverty we have around here—people could have everything they really need."

"It's still only a beginning," Diana said. "There are other things we need much more than money."

Dark November drew to a close; the first of December came, and with it the first heavy snow of the year. The view from inside the dome was magnificent, with the dancing whiteness all around and the electric excitement in the air that comes with the first big snow. Kirk got into his suit and went for a walk. He couldn't feel the snow on his face, but it was a pleasure to watch it fall; he went into a clump of spruce that grew not far from the plant, and in that dark quietness where snow sifted down among the rigid branches, covering the brown carpet of the pine needles, he stood and listened to the natural simple noises, a faint breath of wind in the treetops above and that almost unhearable quick light patter of the first snow striking branches, needles, and the ground.

Christmas came, and they had a beautiful Christmas tree in the middle of the park area beneath the dome. The family houses in the plant had their individual Christmas trees, but there were very few children, only a few very small ones who leavened the lump, as Kirk's father used to say. Children belong with Christmas and it's a dull and sad one without them around. Kirk visited the Martins and Anne. They had a tree in the living room, nicely lighted, beautifully decorated, and all the traditional, comfortable, happy decorations of Christmas. But there too the same lack was felt. The Martins' house was without the warmth of children at Christmas. It was a quiet and happy time all the same.

Kirk and Anne went skiing over the Christmas holidays. They chose a particularly lovely day, crisp, cold, not too much above zero but with very little wind. The sun was incredibly bright in the sky of deepest blue. As they rode up the chair lift, the shadows of trees within the woods were as blue as blue. At rifts in the forest, Kirk could gaze out over endless miles of forest and mountains and snow. Hoarfrost whitened every branch of the trees near the top of the mountain and made a lovely tracery, with the sun beyond them and the steel-blue sky close to the horizon, glittering its light particles through every fairylike gathering of the frost.

Kirk could ski reasonably well for a man without much experience, but he saw that he would never be able to touch Anne Martin. She was a wild and elusive flame on the slopes, perfectly controlled, hardly seeming to move her body as she hurtled and moved and zipped and turned. Kirk followed, blundering along, his skis getting wide apart at times. He managed to stay in sight because Anne stopped and waited or zigzagged about the slopes, laughing, hair blowing free, eyes sparkling, cheeks flushed. She was the happiest that he had ever seen her. He was determined that they would ski together often if this was the effect on Anne. When the lift stopped, he and Anne, having skied themselves weary, went inside the lodge to change their boots.

"I hate to go back down," Anne said. "I could stay up here and ski forever."

Kirk groaned. "I could stay up here with you forever, but I don't know if I could keep skiing all the time or not." His legs hurt and his shoulders hurt and a few bumps here and there hurt where he had taken headlong spills in the snow. But the hurt was good and Anne's laughter and her smiles were both good too.

During the fourth week in January, Kirk awoke early one afternoon. He looked out through his window that faced the lake and the mountains, and saw almost nothing. The dark, gray day had closed down. It was raining; fog shrouded the mountains and drifted over the lake, added to by the constant steam rising from the warm water; vapor drifted everywhere and moisture beaded the outer surface of the dome.

"January thaw," Carl Dundee said cheerfully in the messroom. "It comes every year during January. It gets warm, rains, makes an awful mess."

Kirk grunted, looking out of the window; it did, indeed, look a mess. He had hoped to go skiing with Anne that afternoon, but skiing or no skiing, he'd at least see her just as soon as he'd eaten his combination breakfast-lunch. He got his ski things on and put his skis in the rack, feeling a little foolish since it was raining as he did so, and drove into Waybury.

When Anne opened the door of her apartment

she was wearing lounging slacks and a sweater. She saw his ski clothes and smiled.

"Why, Kirk, I guess I should have telephoned you, but I thought you'd realize that it's doing the same thing up on the mountain and skiing wouldn't be much fun."

"I thought so," Kirk said, "but I didn't want to take a chance on missing a ski trip. Anyway, these clothes are comfortable."

"Well, come in," Anne said. "We'll build a fire in my fireplace and we can have some tea and a pleasant time here. There's not much to do outdoors in this kind of weather."

"All nature weeps," Kirk said.

"Yes, that's right."

The little apartment was comfortable and warmly decorated and equipped. The fireplace was unusual, but this had been a large house that had been converted to several apartments.

Kirk got the kindling and the paper and put the logs on the andirons in the fireplace. He struck a match and soon, to balance the grayness of the day, the sloshing of rain against the window panes, and the distant cry of wind, they had the cheerful, heart-warming crackling of a wood fire. Kirk had had lunch not too long before, but when Anne brought out a tea tray with sandwiches, cookies, and cheese he joined in with enthusiasm. The warmth, the closeness, the feeling of being shut in against the weather that cried outside the windows brought them closer together. Kirk sat on the floor before the fire. Anne was sitting by him, leaning against him, but the suit was so slick that her head kept sliding down.

"I can't get comfortable," she said. "You're like leaning against a hunk of glass."

Not inside, Kirk thought. "Well," he said, "why don't you put your head in my lap? It won't fall off of there." She looked at him—he couldn't tell whether she colored or not in the firelight—smiled, and nestled down cozily. The hell with it, Kirk thought, and slipped off his left glove and stroked her hair gently with his bare hand. Lost in thoughts of her own, gazing into the fire, Anne didn't notice that his hand was not gloved. Kirk was biting his lip. He almost couldn't keep it in. He didn't think he could keep it in much longer. He was going to have to tell this girl that he loved her. But what in the world could come of that? What next? There was only one possible solution, if love was ever to be other than frustration for them. Anne could not become a Normal. No device of technology or medicine or anything that man had yet discovered could change a Robert to a Normal once that ugly orange R commenced to show. So if there was ever to be anything for them, he must become a Robert. The physical danger frightened him, of course, but it was more than that. It was shutting himself from so much of the world. If he visited his home again it would have to be in a suit. If he traveled it would have to be in a suit. He could go no further up on his job, and ambition is not a bad or a weak element in a young man's composition.

"I'm surprised you never married, Anne," Kirk said, wondering why he'd picked on this subject; perhaps the same way that one bites on an aching tooth.

She turned and looked up at him, unsmilingly. "I think I never will marry, Kirk," she said very sadly.

"Why not?"

"Because if I'm married, I want the two children that I can have, and Kirk, have you ever seen the Deforms? Even the ones like William, the one with the one leg? I can't bear the thought of having a child like that. I have had friends who have had the terribly deformed children and they have never recovered from it. Kirk, I'm so terrified of having children like that; even poor little Adam. We might have, I might have, an Adam, a big-headed child. There are more of them all the time, you know; they are gradually increasing. Oh, I know they're very lovable, and I adore Adam, and there's something strange there. There is something unusual in the bigheads, but they're going to be so lonely. I would want my children to look like you, to look like their father."

She turned her face away and Kirk was sure, in spite of the firelight, that her face was a little rosier than it had been a moment before. This slip of hers strongly affected him. He put his other arm around Anne, leaned down, unzipped his helmet, and kissed her on the cheek. She was startled.

"Kirk, what are you doing? Are you taking your budget time now? You've already had your half hour."

"Oh, blow it all," Kirk said. "I don't care, Anne, I just don't care."

She only looked at him with such an unutterable sadness and longing in her face that a fist closed within him and squeezed and he knew pain.

"Anne," he said, "I've been considering becoming

a Robert myself. I could take off my suit a little bit each day, take the course of shots. Dr. Carter says he thinks it can be done without . . ."

Anne lifted her face from his lap, turned over, got on her knees, and looked at him, her eyes flashing, her face half sad, half angry, crumpled.

"No, I forbid you to!" she said, then: "I mean, if you do, Kirk, I'll never see you again. *You must not do it!* I won't conceal the fact that I would like to see more of you, and I would like for us to be able to be together. But you *must* not do that. New Roberts have a much higher cancer rate than those who have grown up as Roberts. I couldn't stand it if you got cancer and I thought I—promise me you won't! Promise me!" she cried. Now she was crying furiously, almost hysterically.

"Anne, Anne!" he said.

"Put your glove back on," she said. "Close your helmet. Promise me that you won't!"

They returned to their former position. She put her head again in his lap, but he had put the glove on now, and they stayed so for a long, long time looking silently into the fire.

A few days later the thaw ended. The weather turned cold and the world was encased in ice. It thawed again, the ice softened, and then it snowed. Within another week, the mountains and then the valley were in winter white, refreshed now from the break in the weather, and sparkling in the sun.

Kirk and Anne skied together every weekend and on any holidays Anne had from school. They were together at other times than these, and Kirk was aware of the pressures building up in both of them. He knew that this thing must be settled, that either they were going to reach a point where they no longer could be together at all because of the intensity of emotions, or something would have to break in another direction.

There came an intensely cold early-February afternoon. The sun shone through a haze of blowing snow and ice-crystal fog; a thirty-mile-an-hour wind brought the subzero temperature down to a chill factor of forty or fifty below zero. Kirk was visiting Anne at her school. During her free period, Kirk and Anne took a small tape recorder and Adam, who came willingly and happily with them, into a vacant classroom. They settled down comfortably, talking among themselves about a dozen subjects, and asking Adam an occasional question, to which he usually either nodded and smiled or shook his head, or simply smiled, looking at them in a strange, crystal-clear kind of way that seemed to Kirk to say "Why do you pretend? Why not say everything?" Of course he knew the seven-year-old child was thinking no such thoughts, but that was the way it made him feel. They placed the tape recorder with its microphone on a small stand between them and then ignored it. Adam gave it one swift glance and smiled again. Anne asked him question after question. Little things, simple things. Add two and two; what is five and five? What is your name? Where do you live? Little questions like that. Some he answered. Once the smile disappeared and he looked at them very strangely.

"Seven and three are ten," he said, "but I'm not ready, I don't like to talk. This way is hard."

That was the most that Anne had ever gotten out of him at one time, and she and Kirk were thrilled and delighted. But for a while afterwards Adam was silent. They fell silent too, sitting there listening to the wind whistle and rush about the glass wall of the room.

Kirk was thinking: Oh, my God, what a lovely girl she is, and what a nice one! His soul was full of agony because there was no cure for a Robert. Is there a cure? he thought desperately. Isn't there some way that she can get to be normal again?

"No darling." It was Anne's voice within him; it seemed to come from inside him now. "There is no cure."

"Then," he said, "I'll become a Robert. I will!" From somewhere within him was Anne's voice. "No. No. You must not, remember you must not! If you do I'll never see you again!"

"But why not?" Kirk demanded with all the intensity within him. "I love you, darling! I love you."

"Oh, Kirk, I love you too, dear. Don't you see that's why you must not become a Robert for me? It would kill me to see you change, because you might become different, or die of cancer, the terror of us all. Oh, Kirk, I couldn't stand that! And children! If I were married, I must have children. Oh, I can't have them! Have you seen some of the worst Deforms, Kirk?"

"But some children are fine, Anne. Many of them are fine. Look at all these wonderful children here. Anne, will you marry me? I love you."

"Kirk, how can you know you love me? You have never touched me. All the time that suit, that well has been there between us."

Kirk got up in a frenzy and reached for his helmet zipper. He heard a cough. He and Anne looked up to see that the door was open and the school principal was looking at them quizzically. Anne turned very red. Kirk felt a sudden shock and then anger that this man had stood there and listened to what was obviously an intimate scene of great intensity between them.

The principal said, "Excuse me, I guess you didn't hear me knock. What on earth are you sitting there staring at each other for and saying absolutely nothing? Are you trying to hypnotize him, Anne?"

"Nothing?" Anne gasped.

"Not for the last five minutes. I was wondering how long you would look at each other like that. Anne, will you come by my office after school this afternoon? I've got some lesson plans to talk over with you. And I do think it's time we made some decision about Adam and the others like him. Hello, Adam," the principal said, smiling.

Adam nodded and smiled back.

"Poor little kid," the principal said. "I wonder if we can ever bring him out of that? I'll see you later, Anne. Come by again, Mr. Patrick." He closed the door and went out.

Kirk and Anne stared wildly at each other.

Kirk's mind was seething. Saying nothing? They had been talking. What did the man mean?

"Oh, I've got it!" cried Anne. She ran to the tape recorder. She pressed the rewind button, let it spin, and turned on play. There was nothing. She spun it further back. Still nothing. She spun it a little further back and there was Adam's voice: ". . . this way is hard."

Their next question followed, then another, and another, followed by silence. Kirk stared at the mechanism in amazement. Fron its speaker came only the reproduced sigh of the wind, a breath, a slight sound as when one's foot hits a chair leg or something, just enough to show that the mechanism was in operation. Then came the sound of a knock, silence, the sound of a door opening, a cleared throat, silence, silence, silence, silence. Then the principal's voice came: "Excuse me, I guess you didn't hear me knock. . . ."

They looked at each other. Coldness, then heat, flashed through Kirk. He looked at Anne, he looked at Adam beside him, and then a strange voice sounded in his mind, as clear and as expressive as if it had been spoken. It was Adam's voice. He knew it, but he knew he was not hearing it with his ears.

"Didn't you want me to do it?" the voice said. "I thought you wanted each other to know what you were feeling. I hope I haven't made you uncomfortable or unhappy."

"Oh, Adam, Adam!" Anne cried. *"Kirk!"*

And Anne and Kirk understood with a clear flash of knowledge and awe running through them that this little boy, this mutation, this Adam was a *beginning!* Anne and John already had expected great powers, but this was not only telepathy but also the ability, in a *seven-year-old,* to transfer thoughts between other minds! Retarded, my God, retarded! Adam's voice: "I am not ready." My God, what will he do when he is ready? Anne's agonized cry flashed through his own mind. She had said, "Perhaps we might have a child like Adam." —had

212

said it in fear, and now perhaps it might be that she could say it in hope, for here was the beginning of a new race! Here was the new man! If there were more of the Adams and they were able to reproduce, and Kirk was somehow sure that they could, there was hope then that the human race had its future after all! He looked at Anne and she at him, and then she ran into his arms and he into hers. Nothing mattered, nothing mattered anymore. They could take every chance.

"But, oh, Kirk!" Anne's fear again. "You mustn't turn! If you died of cancer, if you—"

And the light, pleasant, certain voice of Adam, whose lips did not move and who only smiled at them clear-eyed and beautifully, sounded within them.

"Miss Anne, he will not get cancer if he changes. He will be all right."

"How do you know, Adam?" Anne asked, staring.

"I don't know how I know. I'm just sure that I *do* know that he won't."

"Anne, did you hear?" Kirk said, and somehow doubt of Adam's certainty did not touch him at all, though the boy was only seven years old. "Anne, darling," he said. He ripped his helmet open and kissed her for the first time. She returned his kiss and he hugged her close to him against his suit, his damned suit, and they embraced.

* * *

For Kirk and Anne, their relationship having reached an emotional crisis and its moment of truth, things moved into a different plane in which

213

each knew the other and where each was confident of mutual love and yet where nothing that was new entered into their lives on the surface. They were together as much as they could contrive it. Kirk continued to be extremely careful about contact and about his suit, because of Anne's still-strong feeling of despair at the thought of his running the dangers of passing over.

In February Kirk was called to New York again for a physical, as Bright had told him he would do. He felt no qualms this time. He felt sure that Mr. Bright was on his side, and there was no danger of not being allowed to return to his post. Further, he was confident that the increased exposure from his doubled budget time hadn't affected him in any way. He had kissed Anne only that one time in spite of constantly recurring temptation.

No board was convened for him this time; there was only the gleaming mechanized office of the doctor. The physical was unusually long and thorough—Kirk was surprised when he looked at his watch afterward and found he had been there for over an hour. There had been a moment of dizziness when he got up from the table. He felt a faint alarm—had he begun to get dirty? But the doctor assured him that he was fine, in excellent condition. Kirk departed happily on a shopping trip for a present for Anne. The next morning he returned home, to Waybury.

Late in that January or early in that February when cold kept the land locked tight and the snow grew grimy with long remaining, it had seemed that the winter would never pass. But February waned and March began to come, with blue

214

shadows on the white and the golden sun, and a sky of deep blue all covered with an air of immense freshness and clarity. The warmth from the sun created a temperature in the mountains that seemed precisely and exactly right. Kirk was invigorated, soothed, calmed, and made conscious of happiness again.

Soon spring was beginning to shower its quiet indications over the country. John Martin looked about him; he could smell it in the air, see it in the increasing red of apple orchard branches and in the full gold of the weeping willow limbs. Spring moved in the red haze of buds over the woods and the increased singing of the chickadees, the wildwood ring of the nuthatch, and the drum of a pileated woodpecker on a dead tree. Every year John was grateful for the return of spring, and each year he wondered if this might be the last. Man had tampered so far that one really could never know when the Silent Spring would come. That thought always sidetracked him, made him remember that great scientist and prophetess, Rachel Carson, who had sounded the first ringing alarm at the end of the first half of the twentieth century. She had been cursed by a million rapacious hogs, blessed by millions of people whose world was to some degree protected by the message of her book, blessed unconsciously by birds and bees and butterflies, by the fish and whales in the ocean, by deer and grouse and robins. Bless her name!—John murmured automatically, as millions of men had long done.

Late in March, Senator Nat Divol of the Vermont congressional delegation, speaking for all the senators and representatives of Robert country, made a sensational address on the floor of the Senate. With it, he presented a document to the President of the United States that requested revolutionary changes in the power structure and the relationships between Roberts and Normals.

When the text of the speech came over the printer at the dome, everybody off watch gathered in the wardroom. The press had not been notified in advance. Therefore the speech wasn't covered live on TV. But as the rows of words slid silently across the illuminated face of the printer, the absorbed audience grew tense. Kirk was with them. To him it was nothing new in itself; it contained all the requirements that his friends had discussed freely with him, with one or two additions. But the fact that it was officially made by the Roberts to the President caused the words to ring more clearly before his eyes and in his brain.

Senator Divol asked for the following things: increased representation for the Robert areas in Congress, where their handful of congressmen were flooded into impotence by the eight hundred and thirty-three Normals in the House, even though this meant modifying the old strict one-man-one-vote principle that had placed the cities in absolute control of the entire country. The Robert states were to receive royalties on power sent out of the state in which the plant was located. The next two appointees to the Supreme Court should be Roberts. Roberts were no longer to be required to have permits to travel in Normal country. All transportation systems and all educational institutions to be required to prepare proper and comfortable living or traveling quarters for Roberts, and to accept proper proportions of Roberts as students, trainees, or customers. The AEC and NRC to be dissolved and reconstituted as one civilian board, with half of its number to be Roberts, and with powermen in an advisory capacity only. Finally, the power companies were to be given a period of three years for a crash program of the utilization of solar power. By the end of three years they must begin to replace nuclear plants with solar plants. No more nuclear plants were to be built.

Sneck waited in fuming silence until the list was completed. Then the dam burst. "Goddamn stupid Roberts! All they want is to bust the whole thing up. Roberts on the Supreme Court! No AEC! No new plants—" He swore steadily and grossly for a full minute. Then he turned on Kirk. "You and your sweet, nice Goddamn Roberts!" he roared. "What do you think of the bastards now?"

"What I've always thought," Kirk said steadily.

"Solar energy! Bah! The damned fools. And you, Patrick, you're worse than any of them. You lousy Robert-lover. Why don't you go see them and talk it over? Congratulate them!"

"That's just what I'll do," Kirk said, his face red, his shoulders twitching with the desire to smash a fist in Sneck's fat face.

"No you won't. You're under hack. Get to your quarters."

"Powerchief Sneck," Kirk said calmly, "may I remind you of Powermaster Bright's letter? You have seen it, and you have received a copy. It authorizes me to spend all the time I want with the Roberts, and orders you to cooperate. Shall we call the powermaster?"

Sneck turned purple, but didn't say a word. Kirk shrugged and left the room, passing among the startled, strained faces. Such a scene was very rare and never publicly played out in a power dome.

As he drove to Waybury, Kirk noted that snow was going fast from the hillside, and bare ground was already showing through in sunny spots. He found John Martin at home and on the sunny carport roof with Gregory, Charley Morgan, Jim Mann, and Joe Ball. They looked excited and happy, all except Gregory, who was chewing his pipestem and scowling. They greeted him warmly. Kirk took the offered bench and turned to John.

"Sounds like you fellows have been talking to Senator Divol," he said.

"Why yes, I guess we have." John grinned. Gregory took his pipe from his mouth. "Not oftener than once a week or so."

"He's an old duck-blind compadre," Jim Mann added. "That's a fine place to get things settled—a duck blind."

"All the same, Kirk," John added. "Don't think that those demands came from just us. They're what Roberts all over the country want. We know that if we don't get them we're really going to turn into second-class citizens, and personally, I think the world will poison itself to death."

"Do you think they'll agree?" Kirk asked.

"Hell, no." Gregory stretched and grinned sourly. "You don't ever see anybody turning loose of power just because somebody asked them to."

218

"I think it's reasonable," Kirk said. "I don't know why they won't accept it."

"We all hope they will." John's simple statement sounded like a prayer.

"They won't," Gregory said, flatly.

From all Robert country the reaction was instantaneous and enthusiastic. Telegrams, letters, telephone calls poured into Washington. There was a feeling in the air that perhaps, at last, things were going to change. The reaction was not quite as quick from Normal country. Many thoughtful people approved of these ideas, but gradually, as news commentators, newspapers, gossip and publicity campaigns bore down, a feeling of fear began to spread. What did the Roberts want, anyway? Of course it was too bad that they were all sick, all radiated, but what did they want to do? Come down here and dirty up clean country? Did they want to be around Normal people all the time? Want to move in where they weren't wanted? Good heavens, if you had them around all the time it seemed even possible that wild young kids might want to marry a Robert. Good heavens, I feel sorry for them too, but would you want your daughter to marry a *Robert?* The reaction began to grow, and those in power, and those they had hired to bring the reaction about and to gauge its strength, and who could measure public sentiment very precisely, were almost ready with an answer.

The power companies threw every ounce of their immense prestige, wealth, and power into a campaign to discredit the Robert demands. The AEC, and its echo the NRC, were ominously silent, beyond one new communique stating that they understood perfectly well the desire of the Roberts to have members on these commissions, but that the nature of AEC–NRC work demanded such constant conference and traveling that it seemed medically inadvisable that any of the members should be Roberts.

Tenseness grew over the land as spring grew over the countryside.

"Me worry?" Greg said to Kirk. "Not a bit. I know what's going to happen. They'll turn it down."

"Normals aren't bastards, Greg," Kirk said, rather hotly. "Almost all of them would like to help the Roberts. Why won't they make the President accept your views?"

"I'll tell you why. Watched much TV lately? We don't get much of the campaign up here, but boy, are they swamped with it in Normal country! The publicity campaign, the public relations effort, the planted news stories, the columns—even comedians' jokes. The telephone campaigns. All of it. You know, boy, way back in 1976, the state of California voted on a referendum that would have halted the spread of nuclear power in the state until it was proven safe, and until they had a means of disposing of the waste. I've read all about it. Every damned power company in the country poured in the money. There was a campaign against the referendum the likes of which had never been seen. They spent money like water, scores of millions of dollars—what the hell, they didn't have to worry. The cost of defeating the referendum was all added to the power bills that the poor damned suckers everywhere had to pay. You couldn't turn

220

on a TV, open a newspaper, read a billboard or a magazine, talk to anyone, do anything, without running headlong into that propaganda. The slick chicks against the proposition managed to get it turned around so that if you were for the limitation of nuclear plants you voted no; if you were for the nuclear plants you voted yes. That kind of crap. It worked. They licked the California referendum." He sighed. "Makes you feel pretty sad, Kirk. It might be one hell of a different world if that referendum had passed. The people still had the power then. They don't now. Even their opinions aren't their own any more."

Three days after this conversation, the President remanded the Robert demands for study and consideration, and possible implementation, to "the government bodies most closely informed on all matters of atomic power—the Atomic Energy Commission and the Nuclear Regulatory Commission."

Gregory roared with laughter. "I told you," he said. "I told you! Jesus Christ, you don't really think they're gonna give it up, do you? And, John, my lad, just exactly how soon do you think the Atomic Energy Commission will bring out a report recommending the acceptance of all our demands?"

"I don't know," John said. "I expect it might be a pretty long time."

"You're goddamn right it will be a pretty long time, and don't you try to wait around, brother, and hold your breath until it happens."

"Okay, I've known it all along, but I think we threw a little scare into them and now we're going to have to scare them worse."

Kirk didn't know about the council of war that

Gregory, John, and a handful of other leading Roberts from the northeast areas held not long after the Roberts' proposals had been relegated to the Atomic Energy Commission for study. It was an informal meeting that would have sounded to an observer in many ways more like a bull session, a group of quiet and friendly men talking quietly together. This was the upper council of the Interstate Hunting and Fishing Association, and at this meeting they decided that they would move, that the plan must go ahead. The action would take place sometime in May, but there was one important matter yet to be decided. The man from New Hampshire, Gerald Gaylord, looked intently at John.

"You say, John, that you believe this young Norm powerman, Kirk Patrick, will help us?"

John rubbed his chin and looked reflectively off at the mountain where a touch of green was spreading among the purplish tinge of buds.

"I think he will. I want you to know that I don't like asking him very much. I feel like a Judas. If I did not completely and absolutely and with my entire mind and heart believe that he and everyone else will be better off if we are successful, I wouldn't ask him!"

"We understand, John," said the man from southern Maine.

Western Maine said, "I feel the same. But we're lucky to have him here if what you say of him is true. He's a trained powerman. He can handle a board. He can handle a plant. He's a Normal who can dismantle that self-destruct mechanism that they put in the plants, to explode if a Robert comes

222

into the control room. So, if he will help us, we must use him."

"I know that," John said.

"Damn right," Gregory said. "He's a good man, and I think he'll help us. But we'd damn well better make a go of it, or he'll really be in Dutch!"

"So will all of us," the man from Maine said.

The days were longer now, and the last drifts of winter began to melt away. After three days of hard, soaking rains, the ice went out. Streams were back full, and Otter Creek spread out in its annual spring invasion of Otter Creek Valley, enriching meadows and harming nothing, because this annual flooding was expected. The birds were back, singing in full chorus. As April moved on toward early May, the northern spring arrived with its revitalization of the spirit that was as magic as the rebirth of nature itself. John stood on his porch looking out to the mountains, to the grass of his lawn with touches of green, to the haze of leaves, feeling the sun warm on his face. Though a confirmed believer in the thing that they were going to do, he felt deep regret that man must always strive against man, even though all around him there stretched a world that, if left unmolested and unpoisoned, seems in May to be that Eden from which Adam and Eve had been thrust to start the long ascent of man to whatever heights he was going to reach—or to whatever depth he was going to descend.

Chapter Ten /

THE RENEGADE

May was a glory over the land. The mountains were newly green and they lifted the eye high into a bright blue sky touched with white clouds. Now and again the clouds were dark and dropped rain in a steady downfall, or perhaps in drifting showers followed by rainbows. Birds were wild with spring and song. Deep drum of woodpeckers, the fishing season announcement of the nuthatch, the occasional squawk of a pileated woodpecker, orioles scattering coins of music about the yard, crows cawing, and the robins piping on the lawns; all these made the season a delight to the ear.

Kirk went off duty whistling. He was going fishing with John that day, and he was excited about it. He had an hour's nap and a solid breakfast. Then he picked up his assembled gear, fly rod, fishing vest, landing net, and a multitude of various objects, useful and otherwise: flies, needlenosed pliers, fly dope, line dope, buckshot, knife, and on and on.

When he arrived at John's he found Anne; she had taken advantage of her morning free to come wish them luck on this first fishing trip of the year. She smiled at Kirk.

"Whenever Dad is getting ready to go fishing he seems ten years younger," she said. "Hear him whistling and humming in there?"

"Sure do. I feel that way myself. Anne, why don't you come?"

"I wish I could. If we weren't having school today, I'd be right with you. You can bet your boots on that." She put two fingers to her lips and pressed them on the clear helmet alongside Kirk's cheek.

"Oh, hell!" he said. "What a way to have to make love!" He grabbed her and pulled her to him. He ripped up the zipper of his helmet and kissed her firmly. Fireworks soared within him as she returned his kiss, her arms around his plastic shoulders. They embraced for a moment and then she stepped away.

"Close that thing, Kirk! Look at this." She held her hand so that the orange R was clear before his eyes. He reached down and covered the R with his two hands, then took her hand and brought it to his lips. Only then did he close his helmet, and she turned and ran so that he couldn't see her cry. He had forgotten about fishing when John said from the door, "Ready to go, Kirk?"

Diana answered her husband from a flower bed where she was beginning operations. "He's been waiting for you for fifteen minutes, you idiot. Of course he's ready."

"I'm all set, John," Kirk said, as cheerfully and calmly as he could.

They went in John's car, with the warm breeze blowing in through the open windows, replete with the smells of spring, warm earth, green leaves, blossoms. Kirk, encased in his suit, could smell nothing and feel nothing of this in actuality, but he saw it with his eyes, and heard it all, and felt it through John's serene face. Gradually the lump of ice that was his heart melted away in the spring sunshine. They left Route 7 at Brandon, wound through farming country and through a covered bridge over Otter Creek. The creek was still high, just barely within its banks. They wound through woods, turned left, climbed, and drove past a pond on the left and a handsome building on the right.

"That's the research center for the reserve," John said. "I'm a trustee."

The road meandered through some more woods and up hills. They left it for a dirt road turning off to the right. The dirt road wound up a high green hill; to the left and below was a handsome small lake with thick woods and a rising mountain on the opposite side, with a small ski area well off to the left.

"What a lovely place!" Kirk exclaimed.

A beautiful house crowned the hill. It wasn't very large, but it was full of personality and balanced beauty. John stopped the car by the front door and went in. He came back shortly with a couple of paddles.

"I telephoned ahead," he told Kirk as he got into the car, "so Andy had the paddles ready. We try to have only one party at a time on the pond, so that a man can be alone here."

They took a woods road from the house. It ran through a gap between two hills and came into a stand of tall white pines that formed a cathedral under the sky. Woods birds were singing, wind

227

was sighing in the upper works of the pines, and the pine-needle-covered ground was warm, with splotches of moving gold on it where the sun filtered through. John pulled off the road and parked. "Here we are," he said. Kirk could hear the excitement and pleasure in the older man's voice. "It's amazing," John went on, "how much junk I bring along everytime I come here." They started taking gear from the car.

By the time they had distributed a plastic, clean-insulated lunch bag, two small folding chairs, cushion life preservers, creels, rods, net, paddles, and the like, they were loaded down.

"No end to it," Kirk said. "If we caught one fish for each piece of gear we'd load the boat."

The pond covered some fifteen or twenty acres, a natural lake in the cup of the mountains, surrounded by woods except for a small open meadow on one side; a large oak tree stood alone there, not too far from the lake. There was no dock, no made structure to reveal man's presence. A canoe was bottom-up beneath a tree where John dumped his part of the equipment. They put the canoe in the water, arranged their belongings, and embarked. John insisted on taking the first turn at paddling.

"Ahhh! This is nice," Kirk said. From up in the woods across the lake came a wild, soft song.

John turned his face toward Kirk. "That's a white-throated sparrow," he said quietly. "My favorite sound in the woods."

Life was everywhere about them. To their left solid woods of spruce, hemlock, white pine, oaks, beech, birch, and popples stretched up a thousand feet to a rock wall that was topped by more trees.

Above the ridge a hawk circled in the air. Birds sang and flew; three ducks took off from the far side of the pond and beat swiftly out of sight. "Woodies!" John said. A constant flow of insect life moved in and above the water. Little clouds of tiny insects danced like thin smoke in the sun.

"Try a nymph, deep," John said. "Here's a good one. Ron Trout tied it. We call it the Bielli Bug—why I don't know." The bait was about half an inch long, hard and solid, with a brown glazed back and a brown-striped yellow underbody, with a little tuft of hair bristling just beneath the eye of the hook and along the curving shaft beneath the body.

"There just might be a hatch later, if it stays warm," John said. "But for now, let's just troll with the nymphs. Better put a small shot on your line so it will sink deep."

Kirk followed directions, and within five minutes something tried to snatch his rod from his hand. He tightened his grip with a violent start. He'd been simply enjoying the beauty of the place and the morning, forgetting the fish.

"He's a good one!" John exclaimed in excitement, as the rod bent nearly double, the tip touching the water until Kirk let the reel run. "Look out! Don't give him any slack. Follow him, Kirk, follow him. Keep the tip up, keep the tip up!"

Kirk fought the fish, managing the line with his left hand, recovering lost line by short, quick pulls, working it through his fingers as the fish swirled around the bow of the canoe and then back again. Kirk could feel the hard savage tugging through the line and rod and his entire body.

"A rainbow would have jumped by now," John said. "Must be a brookie."

"Quite a brookie!" Kirk said, filled with an agonizing suspense. He was using a light leader and a three-ounce rod and the fish felt like a whale. Deep in the clear water he saw the fish, a nice trout, fighting, tugging, his body flashing in reflected sunlight as he turned. Gradually, sweating and excited, Kirk worked the fish in alongside the canoe. John missed with the first dip of the landing net, and the frightened fish surged down again, taking the line. Kirk worked him back gingerly, hoping the hook would hold, the leader wouldn't break, the canoe wouldn't sink, lightning strike, or a tornado hit, not before he had landed this fish! Up again. John slipped the net under the trout, and brought him into the canoe, a very nice fourteen-inch brook trout. Kirk whooped like an Indian, staring at the dark back, the tiny blue-centered red dots, the red-orange belly. The fish was wholly beautiful, fresh and cold from clean cold water, gleaming in the sun.

"Damn it!" John said ruefully. "I've gotten to where I even hate to kill a fish."

"Put him back," Kirk said. This fish was too beautiful to kill and eat.

"No," John said. "I don't want to get maudlin about this. I certainly wouldn't take very many of these trout. As soon as we have all we want to eat, I'll put any others back. A fish really doesn't have much of a future anyway. Somehow it's not the same as killing a bird or a deer."

They fished on and caught several more very nice trout. One two-pound rainbow gave John a battle for at least five minutes. Then John pointed the canoe for the right hand bank. They pulled up by a ledge from which the water dropped sharply into clear blue depths. They tied the canoe, handed out their gear, and then climbed out and set up housekeeping on the sunlit ledge, thick with pine needles, topped by a hemlock. They were right beside the clear water and in the warm sun. John opened the insulated bag.

"I hope you saved some budget time, Kirk, so you can have some lunch. Everything here is clean."

"I certainly have," Kirk said.

"Okay, start off with this cold beer." The can, which would disintegrate within twenty-four hours after being emptied, was cold against his lips. The icy beer tasted wonderful going down. So did the sandwiches, cake, and the coffee from a thermos. After lunch they lounged in the two chairs, and Kirk appreciated their comfort. John smoked a pipe.

"Keeps the bugs off," he said.

John puffed at the pipe and blew a cloud of blue smoke into the spring air. He looked over at Kirk.

"Something I've always wondered. Every power-man I've talked to before was convinced that the power companies are perfect, and could stand no talk against them. You're not that way at all. How come?"

"Inherited, I guess," Kirk said. "My father isn't at all sold on the present system; his grandad talked to him a lot about how things used to be before the nuclear plants took over the country. When my great-grandfather was a kid in Kentucky, way back, the Kentucky-Tennessee Light and Power Company sent crews out all over Kentucky and Tennessee, armed with shotguns, and they just about wiped out the big white, black, and red woodpeckers that used to be so common, and are only now making a comeback. They even went into bird sanctuaries, parks, everywhere, and shot them."

"The bastards!" John said, with feeling.

"Dad thought it was arrogant, thoughtless, and vicious. But the power companies have always been like that, always been arrogant, always ready to run over people's rights, destroy land, destroy anything. Great-grandad also told Dad that power companies in Louisiana were, at the same time, paying a bounty for pileated woodpeckers. Brought them to the very edge of extinction."

"Why, in the name of God?"

"Same as with the other woodpeckers. They thought the birds were damaging power poles, telephone poles. I can't see how; no one can, but some bastards decided that woodpeckers shouldn't peck on power-company poles. So they wiped them out."

"Typical," John said. "They have, of course, done a thousand times worse since then, but somehow that seems so damned vicious, so wholly nasty. It should have been a warning to people. But I suppose not very many noticed it."

"Great-grandpa Patrick did," Kirk said. "He shot one of the power-company hunters in the seat of the pants with a .410 shotgun, and *his* dad threw them off the place."

"But you joined them," John said, quizzically.

"If you can't lick 'em, join 'em."

"Maybe, then, we don't have to join them." John blew another cloud of smoke and reached for a match.

A few gnats danced about them, but the sun and breeze kept the spring time no-see-ums and black flies away. Circuses of tiny insects danced above the water. A dragonfly whipped by now and then close against the surface, dipping her long tail in the water at intervals, touching off eggs. Little water spiders skittered on the surface, disturbing the patterns of the water bugs. A hatch of small mayflies came into the sun. Life was everywhere, and the whitethroat whistled again, and a vireo answered from the deep woods.

Kirk sighed in contentment and sat back. "It certainly is wonderful, John."

For a moment, John's face was very old. He shook his head and said, "Kirk, I've got to tell you something. We need your help."

"Sure," Kirk said, looking at him. "I'll be glad to do anything I can, anytime. You know that."

"This is a bigger thing than you can possibly think, Kirk. We Roberts have a plan. You were right when you thought we had talked to the senator who made the Roberts' demands to the President."

"I was sure of it—it sounded so much like you and Greg and Joe and the others."

"Yes. Well, we are now convinced that the Normals will never act on those demands, so we're going to take some action to shove them along a little."

"You are?" Kirk sat up straight, the beauty of the

day fading a little. "You sound serious. What are you going to do? Everybody write the President? Start your own political party?"

"No, it's going to be worse than that," John said solemnly. "We are organized. We are in touch with Roberts all over the country. We're going to show by action, which will be followed by Roberts everywhere, that we simply are not going to let things continue as they are now."

"How are you going to do that?"

"We're going to cut the lines to your plant, and all the power lines taking electricity from Robert country."

"What?" Kirk cried, lunging to his feet. "Cut the lines from *my* plant! What good will that do?"

"A notification to all Normals that we Roberts can, if we must, upset everything. Then we want to take over the plant, so that we in Vermont and New Hampshire will have enough power for essentials. You don't know it, Kirk, but Charlie Morgan has perfected our own shot serum. He makes it from the venom of the larger honeybees. We think it is even better than that made in Normal country, and we have enough for a year. With one plant to give us power, we are independent, and I don't think that this country has gone so far along the road to tyranny that it will send troops. All Robert country will support us, and I believe that with this demonstration of what we Roberts *could* do, they will come around. You know our demands are reasonable."

"But this is a revolution!" Kirk said, shocked.

"In a way. There have been other revolutions. All I can say is, Kirk, that we have every hope and every intention that it will be bloodless and without violence, a revolution that will benefit both sides, in the long run. You know what we want. Don't you really agree that our demands are right and just?"

"Yes. I do. I can't understand why the President didn't accept them."

"Power," John said, sadly. "Gregory is right, people who have power and a thirst for it don't relinquish power willingly. Still, the change must come someday, and we've decided that it must come now, before more of the earth is lost to radiation. The most essential thing is the development of solar energy."

"Yes," said Kirk, uncertainly. He tried to quell the double in his brain. "I know you showed me your energy cells and I saw them working. I put an ammeter and a voltmeter on them, and I know how much power those few cells were putting out. Are you *sure* they've been working for thirty years? We have always been told it was more like thirty minutes, and then they fused out."

"Would I lie to you, son?"

"No, sir." Kirk was ashamed, touched by the sadness of his friend's voice. "But someone might have tricked you, might have . . ."

John shook his head. "Nope. Not a chance. They were put in and sealed soon after we built the house. And I'm not the only one that has them."

"But materials—are they . . . ?"

"Common as dirt—sand. And power. Our experts, and we have some, Kirk, can't imagine that they will not work with equal efficiency in much larger

235

sizes. And certainly better in more sunstruck areas than Vermont!"

"It is such an enormous change, John."

"Yes. But we have domes on the moon and on Mars, with men living in them. Wives rocketing up to join them. You know as well as I that if this society really starts to exploit solar power with all the resources that it has—why, good God, Kirk, there is no limit! The power companies and the power structure of this country remind me in a wry, uncomfortable sort of way of the Catholic Church. Created for the vast benefit of mankind, the structure has become so dogmatic about its ideas and itself as institution that it now impedes the real progress of mankind. It is a strange parallel, but a rather true one."

Kirk smiled, though he didn't really feel very much like it. "Ohm's law," he said wryly. "The right-hand rule. I is equal to E over R. Yes, I guess we have our revelations, our scripture." The thought that he had been about to pursue returned to him. He studied John's face—rather round, not very bony, clear blue eyes, tanned face wrinkled, brown gray-shot hair getting pretty damned thin in front and on top.

"Look, John. How can you possibly take over the plant when you . . . when . . ." He stopped. The self-destruct mechanism was not a very commonly known matter. The power companies tried to keep it as quiet as possible, even if only as a matter of public relations.

"You mean about the mechanism that blows up the plant if a Robert comes into the board room?"

"Yes."

236

"You know," John said thoughtfully. "The presence of that destruct mechanism really angers me. It angers all of us. It is the ultimate comment on what the power companies really feel toward the people they have nearly destroyed. I understand that the explosion is supposed to wreck only the control and cooling systems. But you can't tell me that a plant disrupted in such a way will not emit vast quantities of radioactive vapor. Long, long ago, a small British plant, one-thousandth the size of yours, blew out its cooling system. Four hundred square miles of crops had to be destroyed. This monster? If it goes it will triple radioactivity in a fourth of Vermont. Punishment, for having dared to tamper with the High Power Companies' 'divine' control over mankind."

"Well," said Kirk, stuttering, for he really didn't believe what he was saying. "I understand there could be some radioactivity released, but it's supposed to be for only a short while, and not very concentrated . . ." He damned well knew better. That core might not melt down and explode, but it would be putting out clouds of radioactive steam and gas for a hell of a long time. . . . The original question returned. "Look, John, whatever you think of it, what are you going to do about it? It is there, it really is, and it's turned on all the time."

John, appearing to be a totally different person, older, lined, almost haggard, just looked at him, his smile totally gone.

"Kirk," he said. "You *know!*"

It was like receiving a stunning blow and a bucket of ice water in the face. Kirk realized that he, a Normal, a powerman with a key to the board, could turn off that destruct mechanism so that the Roberts could take over the plant. But did they really think that he would do that? He, Kirk Patrick, betray himself, his country, his company, his plant? He could feel anger surging up in him.

"Is this, then," he said coldly, "why you have been so good to me? Why the Roberts have been my friends?"

"No!" said John, his voice harsh and hard. "No. The friendship came first, the liking came first. Everything came first, before we decided we could ask you to help us. You know that I, today, have placed all of us totally in your hands. But we trust you."

This softened his anger a little, but it was still there. No man likes to be used. Was he being used? Was he? He thought of Anne, her face, her softness, her gentleness and warmth. Could she . . .

"Is this why Anne . . . ?" he began harshly.

John leaped to his feet and shouted: "No!" He pounded his right fist into his left hand, then wrung them. "I was afraid you might think that. Anne does not know that we plan to use you, that we want you to help us. She knows we have some kind of a plan; she knows about our ideas, she knows what we want to do. But she does not know what we are asking you to do! I have been afraid to tell her, even though I wanted to. I am certain that she would have tried to wreck the whole thing. No, Kirk. I have worried about this, but you must believe me, that this has nothing to do with you and Anne."

"I see," Kirk said, a little bitterly. He sat down

and looked out over the lake, his mind spinning. At the moment he hated John and the other Roberts. He almost hated Anne. But he couldn't really hate them, certainly not Anne, love for whom ached all through him. Anne! he thought. Then he thought of his parents, his career, and of the future. It seemed an impossible thing that they asked of him. John was watching him. The anger and hardness gone from the older man's face, and Kirk could see the sympathy in his eyes.

"Kirk, if we succeed, you won't be throwing away your training and ambition. A part of our terms will be that you be retained by your company and not penalized in any way. Actually, I think that under the new system that must be set up, you will be doubly important to them. I think it will enhance your career eventually, not destroy it. If we succeed."

"*If* you succeed. A big if, John."

John nodded. "It's not very much to offer you, son. I know there is a good chance of failure. But whatever happens, we will always and forever stand behind you."

Kirk's emotions were in turmoil, but his mind was beginning to clear. He knew that what these people wanted was right and good for everyone. He was sure now that solar energy was practicable with three years of intense and concentrated research, with all the facilities of government, science, and the power companies totally involved. If solar energy was made useable, there would lie, over the years, the physical salvation of the world, the power to clean up the planet.

Suddenly the day was beautiful, golden, and

green about him. He looked up at John, remembering all his life behind him and wondering what was to lie before.

"All right, John," he said. "I'll do it."

They discussed the plan then. On the chosen day, Kirk would turn off and dismantle the self-destruct mechanism at six in the morning, one half hour before his relief. At that precise moment, three of the Roberts who worked in the plant would open the outer door. A group of Roberts would then come into the plant, take it over, and ship the Normal staff off to Normal country. The power lines to Normal country would be cut only as a symbol, a demonstration of what the Roberts could easily do. The power lines were very vulnerable, very exposed, and easily repaired.

If everything went as planned, there should be no violence at all, which was what the Roberts prayed and hoped for.

They took the fish home through a world that Kirk hardly saw now. Though John asked him to come in when they arrived at his house, Kirk begged off, saying he had better get back to the plant. John nodded.

"I understand, Kirk. Some parts of this day, I enjoyed."

"Yes, same here."

"I see Anne's car, so she must be here."

"I know. But I think . . . I think I had better go."

John's serenity showed no flaw as Kirk got into his car with his gear and drove away. Kirk wondered if John thought that he was going back to the plant to reveal the plot. He wondered a little bit himself.

The rest of that week was a blur. He saw none of the Roberts for two or three days; then, not wanting Anne to realize that something was wrong, he made a date with her, and they drove together to Burlington to see a new movie. It was a little hard for Kirk when he met Anne. He didn't mention the plot or his part in it, nor did she. He was sure John had not told her, even now. He looked into her clear eyes, listened to her talk and laugh, and kept his gloved hand on hers. And he was positive that she didn't know. He thanked God that she didn't, for it was a thing that might have come between them always. Of course she knew that her father and his friends were planning something to make the federal government accept their demands, but she probably thought only of political action.

The weekend crept by. He went fishing with John again on Monday, this time in a clear trout stream. He thought John had something to say to him, and for the first time in his life he saw a good trout strike at his dry fly without feeling any emotion at all.

John did have something to say.

The day was to be the following Thursday.

Kirk didn't even know he was on a trout stream. He didn't feel the rod in his hand or hear the burble and splash of running water or the redwing that was chattering softly in the tree above. Thursday. Three days. What would they have done if he refused? What would they do now if he refused? Drop the whole thing, most likely. This thought

241

shook his resolution. He saw that John was watching him narrowly. Only the fact of his confirmed trust and confidence in these Roberts allowed him to agree to continue. He believed, wholly, that they did not want to destroy or disrupt society, but rather save that society, save mankind and the planet, prevent all life from dying in the increasing radiation that would envelop the world in the end.

Suspense grew in Kirk until by Wednesday he found it difficult to remain still, sitting or standing, almost impossible to eat, and his sleep was haunted by forebodings and his awakenings by a sense of deepest guilt and misery. He found that only the thought of Anne could ease this guilt and dread; he began to realize the bind he really was in. For if he failed the Roberts, and thus Anne and perhaps the world, would not his entire life, wherever it led, be one of guilt and remorse? It seemed to him that he had only a choice between two nightmares; he could only pick the least bad.

Anne's presence was more effective than his thoughts of her; with her he could at least sit fairly quietly and talk, forgetting the coming crisis. But he could not hide his tenseness, his nervousness, or quiet the shaking of his hands, not even with her. She showed a very obvious surprise, puzzlement, and finally deep concern over his condition.

"What is it, Kirk?" she asked him on Wednesday afternoon when he was beginning to feel that for him death might be the only way out of the dilemma. "What's wrong, dear? You look unwell, you seem so nervous. Are you sick?"

"No, dear," he said, looking into her face, feeling

his misery lightening due to her concern. And due to her puzzlement, too, for here, surely, was the final complete confirmation of the fact that she had not led him on to be used for the Roberts' aims. Had she known what he was planning to do the next morning, she would have understood his condition.

"Then what is it? Can't you tell me?"

He told her that it was the old problem that gnawed at him. She was a Robert, she was radiated; he was a Normal. He saw the renewed agony in her eyes as he talked, and longing swept over him. Why could he not have her? Was there no way out?

"Anne, darling," he said. "I love you. Why not let me join you?"

"No!" she said in horror. "No, you must not!"

"But Anne. Remember little Adam? Don't you see that he is the new man? That he and others like him may create a new human race? By the time he and the others are grown, only God knows what they will be able to do."

"I know," sobbed Anne. "It's not that. I'd love to have an Adam! Kirk, did you know that he, and all of them, are absolutely conditioned against violence and cruelty? That they cannot stand the sight of any living thing being mistreated, and will only turn to violence themselves to stop cruelty?"

"Yes. Then what is it, Anne? Why can't I join you?"

"Cancer," she whispered. "And you are clean, Kirk, *clean!* I won't have you give that up for a future with me. Suppose I let you, and you died? No, Kirk, no!"

They sat silently together for a time, each sunk in the dilemmas that lay before them.

When he left, he opened his helmet and kissed her good-bye; it was only the third time he had kissed her, and he wondered dully if it would be the last. It was a brief kiss, for she refused to cling to him very long.

He returned to the plant, having tried to eat dinner at the Waybury Inn. He could hardly swallow his food, and he resisted fiercely the impulse to drink and drink until torment dulled and perhaps went away with oblivion. He drank nothing and ate little. He knew he could not endure the last supper with his colleagues at the plant. Concern had been expressed to him already by Carl Dundee, and Mary Owen had spent half an hour the afternoon before urging him to see a doctor.

After he had driven his car into the plant dome, he kept on his suit and went for a walk. The moon was high, nearly full, and the mountain and lake made a black and silver picture that took some of the pain from his heart.

"Going out again, Mr. Patrick?" the guard asked as he approached the lock.

"Just for a little walk, Mike," Kirk said, surprised at the easy normalness of his voice. He had doubted his ability to speak at all.

"A grand night for it, that's for sure," Mike said.

Kirk walked for an hour in the woods and along the lake, and the lovely world, the tainted world that was sick with the inner illness of radiation, soothed him and made him again feel hope. If he could save it, keep it as beautiful as it was, then every sacrifice was worthwhile.

The night. The board. Duty. The hours that seemed to hurtle by and yet seemed to drag through lifetimes. The comparative serenity of his walk in the moonlight had gone far away from him. He hated the act that he must commit. He was a loyal man by nature. The thought of betraying the Normals, the company, his parents, grated on his nerves like sandpaper on tender skin. He could not have done it had he not been convinced that it really wasn't betrayal—though he knew that that would be the word they would use. Traitor! Renegade!

When the clock began to strike six, Kirk was standing by the tiny red door in the center of the Board. Before the clock had finished striking he had his key—*his key!* (*Wear it with honor and faith.*) in his hand.

His trembling fingers could barely guide the key into the keyhole. He turned it, hesitated, and opened the red door. Inside was a small box, painted red. A red-capped switch was on its front; it was pushed to the right to *On*. Kirk reached in. His hand touched the switch and involuntarily jerked away. He could hear his heart beating; it sounded like distant thunder. His breath whistled in his lungs.

He pushed the switch to the left, to *Off*.

He closed the door and locked it, his hands so wet that he almost dropped the key. He hung the key around his neck again, and went back to the powerman's seat, thinking to himself that no matter what John had said about the future, this was probably the last time he would sit in the powerman's chair before a board of power.

His feeling of remorse and guilt, his gnawing desire to open the red door again and undo what he had done, his mixed feelings of hope and despair and guilt, and hope again, all these were shattered when the door to the control room smashed open and Sneck, Frank Owen, and three of the guards appeared in the room.

"Arrest him!" Sneck ordered harshly. Mike, his face contorted because he thought of Kirk as a friend, and another guard took Kirk's arms. Kirk didn't try to struggle. He stood quietly, each arm held fast. Sneck looked at him with hate in his red face. He went to the board, opened the red door and looked inside. Then he turned to Kirk, his mouth hard as slate, his thick lips compressed to a white line. "It's turned off," he said.

Frank Owen said, "Oh my God, Kirk!"

Sneck stopped glaring and his face paled. He looked at Kirk intently, his small eyes narrow lidded. "Even when I was told I didn't believe it! You bastard. You goddam renegade!" He reached in through the door, and Kirk heard the click of the switch as the destruct mechanism was turned on again. Sneck closed and locked the door. He strode over to Kirk, tore open the collar of his uniform and jerked key and chain from around his neck.

"I gave it to you," he snarled. "And I'm taking it back. You're all done, Buster, all done. Finished. Stupid jerk. I can tell you because you're not going to have any chance to pass it on—they've got special rules for treason, Buster. Power Academy graduates are under military law, Patrick. Think about it. In every plant, Buster, among the

Roberts, there is a Normal from Security. He looks like a Robert; he acts like a Robert, except that he's quartered in the Dome. He's there to find out what's going on. And he told us. The two Roberts who were going to open the gate are locked up. The gates are locked and sealed. No one goes in or out. A chopper from Security will be here any minute to take you back. Okay, you guards. Hang onto Patrick and bring him along. We'll let his Robert friends outside the gate get a look at him!"

All male Normals in the plant were on guard outside, armed with pistols, faces strained, facing the main gate. All nuclear plant employees were reservists and received regular training each year; there was a military precision in their line, though they had not donned their uniforms. Kirk saw the women over at one side. Mary Owen was crying. Sneck and the two guards led Kirk before the double rank of armed men and to the gate. Inner and outer gates were of straight, transparent plastic, allowing clear visibility both ways. A group of perhaps forty or fifty men were standing outside the gate. They wore green shirts and carried deer rifles. The Green Mountain Boys ride again, Kirk thought bitterly and in despair. For him it would be death, of course; for his parents it would be disgrace. For his friends? Unless they gave up and simply left, many of them might be killed, especially when the Security chopper arrived, with its battery of machine guns. Even so, the leaders would be hunted down and charged with interfering with power, a serious offense that could bring years of imprisonment.

The group outside came close to the gate, staring

in. With a shock, even though it was expected, Kirk recognized John, his face a dirty white. Gregory was chewing his pipe. Joe Ball, Jim Mann, and Charley Morgan were in the front rank. They stood there looking through the closed transparent gate, staring at Kirk, their faces impassive. Sneck spoke; his voice, carried outside by the PA system, echoed all through the dome as well.

"We have Patrick," Sneck said in iron tones. "The destruct mechanism is set. Patrick will be tried for treason. You are done for! If you try to break in or blockade us, we will destroy the plant. Now, you lousy Robert bastards! Get the hell out of here and quit cluttering up company property. Get!"

Kirk saw defeat mirrored in the well-known faces before him. Then he saw John's face twitch in sudden alarm, then startled panic. John turned around and lifted an arm, shouting something. At that precise moment a distant explosion sounded, reverberating from the mountain, echoing inside the dome. A siren started a shrieking mournful wail from the main building and a gong began clanging from the living quarters. At the same time, the sound caught clearly up by the mikes outside the gate, came to the rhythmic flailing sound of a helicopter. Kirk looked up and saw it in the sky overhead—white, marked with the crossed lightning of the power combine—with machine gun muzzles pointing in clusters from its sides.

"My God!" Sneck shouted. "They've cut the lines! That does it. Plan B, Owen, Dundee! We'll get out of here and blow the plant!"

Kirk caught his breath. Plan B! The destruct

248

mechanism would be set to function at a given time. All the crew would evacuate by car and personnel carrier. If any Robert tried to enter the control room before the explosion, it would be triggered instantly.

The operation took only minutes, for all the Normals knew exactly what must be done. Kirk had participated in drills like this himself, back in training, scornful because he knew it could never happen, either by design or by accident. Within minutes, all the cars and trucks were lined up before the main airlock. The two Robert guards who had been going to open the gate were handcuffed in a van. The siren screamed on and on, the gong clanged, the serenity and precision of this well-ordered place was shattered, lost, gone perhaps forever.

Kirk was placed in the back seat of the first car, with Sneck beside him, revolver in hand. Two guards were in the front seat. Through the car's transparent bubble he saw Mary Owen crying as she looked at him; then Frank was moving her away to another car.

"All right, Patrick," Sneck said bitterly. "Proud of yourself? This plant will blow in ten minutes, after the chopper has picked us up at the pad. I've set the destruct for maximum damage, so that the cooling system will be ruptured and the dome broken. There's going to be a hell of a lot of radioactive vapor around here mighty soon. Anybody without a suit will get a hell of a dose—too much for the goddamn shots to handle. But that's their lookout."

Kirk thought frantically, desperately, why don't

they stop us. Grab Sneck, take off his suit—he'd probably run back in there and turn off the destruct. . . . They could destroy us all, there are enough of them, but they won't, they won't. They're not harsh enough to do it! Sneck was beside him now, bellowing for the last man to open the gate. Ten minutes. Suddenly, like a cold wave rushing away from him, all guilt for what he had tried to do vanished forever. The Normals could have stayed here and held the plant until relieved. There was no need to blow it, to add a heavy concentration of radiation to this area. He looked out of the car and through the transparent dome at the people before the gate and he saw with horror that a girl was there. A girl! My God! Anne! She was crying desperately.

"It's Anne!" he shouted. "It's Anne, and she has no suit! None of them have suits. If this place goes she'll be killed. Sneck—George, you can't do this. You can't! Tell them the place will go up in ten minutes!"

"I doubt that they can get far enough away," Sneck said coldly. "They should have cut the lines. This will be a lesson to the Roberts!"

Inner and outer gates opened together, a red light came on in the lock, and another siren began to sound as airtight integrity was broken. The car moved through the gate and the Roberts fell back before it. Kirk saw his friends, saw Anne's agonized face, and shouted: "Get out, get out! The plant will blow up in ten minutes!"

Some of them fell back, some more of them started to run. He saw John and Anne as the car moved past. They were standing there, arms around each other. He saw Gregory swearing and shaking a fist at the car. He was aware that Sneck had a gun at his head, plainly visible from outside, and knew that was why his friends didn't rush the car.

Kirk swung his right arm and shoulder, all his weight behind the looping, heavy blow. His fist knocked Sneck's gun aside and thudded against the powerchief's jaw, slamming him heavily against the side of the car. In the same motion, Kirk lashed a kick with his right foot with all his strength against the turned and startled face of the right hand guard. Then Kirk was diving head first across the seats, hearing a curse and ejaculation from the driver. Kirk's left hand hit the wheel and jerked, while his right speared down and pressed the accelerator pedal to the floor. Like a spurred horse the powerful electric car lunged ahead with neck-snapping acceleration. Kirk felt blows on his head, but the driver was wrestling too hard with the wheel to hit very effectively, and with no time to draw his gun. Kirk yanked the wheel a last desperate time, keeping the acceleration pedal well down, feeling somebody in the back seat grab his legs. Sneck!

With a crash the car slammed into a tree. The impact drove Kirk half-unconscious against the front of the car, which reared up again like a horse before dropping to its wheels. Kirk made his dazed brain work. Sneck had turned loose of his feet. He swung them up and over the unconscious guard on the right, broke away from the dazed man at the wheel, wrestled the door open, hearing the hiss of released air, and lunged out into the day. He heard car horns, shouts, shots! Hands reached to free him, and yet another car pulled up with brakes screeching, guards leaping out of it. They grabbed Kirk. He tore free as one of them doubled over, grasping his stomach, and fell heavily. Then a group of green-shirted Roberts hit the guards. The chopper came over with a crescendo of noise and the madness of its airstream. Its machine guns dazzled the day with noise and flame. Kirk saw a swathe cut through the mass of Roberts as they ran for the car. Then half a dozen men knelt with deer rifles spitting. Kirk saw Gregory among them. The chopper whirled up, around, its blades vertical, clawing. It fell over forward and crashed, then exploded. Other guards were down. The fight was savage and, for the moment, merciless and a kaleidoscope of action. Kirk saw Roberts wielding rifles like clubs, revolvers spitting, Roberts and Normals going down. He saw Sneck down, with Gregory Mainyard kneeling on his chest. For a moment things were in doubt. Then forty or fifty more Roberts arrived at a run, and all action ceased. The instant silence that followed was broken only by the groans and cries of wounded men and the crackling of flames where the helicopter burned. Kirk felt sick, but there was no time to mourn now.

"The key, the key!" Kirk shouted, pointing at Sneck. "He has my key inside his shirt!"

Sneck, with a convulsive effort, threw Gregory aside and started to get up. Gregory grabbed his arm and shoulder and flipped the big man over and down on his back. Gregory was on him like a cat, a knife flashing! "No!" Kirk shouted. The knife swooped down and slit Sneck's suit from waist to neck. Sneck screamed. He was unhurt, but Kirk knew he had a terrible fear of radiation, of being exposed to this dirty air.

Most of the ten minutes were up!

Gregory wrenched the key chain from around Sneck's neck. Kirk grabbed it and ran for the plant as he had never run before, shouting over his shoulder, "Anne, get out! John, get Anne away, run, run, run! It will go in three minutes!"

Kirk dashed through the open air lock, just as the inner door was swinging shut, controlled by the timed closing device. Had they locked the main building? Could he make it? The siren was wailing and wailing above; the one at the gate had ceased, but the gong clanged on above the living quarters. Kirk was inside the main building, racing for the control room. Only seconds left, only seconds. The red door was before him, the key was in his shaking hand, he could not fumble, could not lose a second, the key wouldn't go in, it went in, he turned it, swung the door open and, with what seemed like horrible slowness, he reached in and flipped the switch to *Off*.

Kirk fell, almost unconscious, over the seat, slipping on down onto his knees. The closing gate had left his friends outside the dome, and he was alone here. He stood up, took a deep breath, and tried to still his trembling hands. He unlocked another section of the board, took a screwdriver and pliers, and removed the destruct mechanism. He disarmed it. He placed it on the bench and sat down. He felt dazed. He had done it, truly he had done it. He was ruined forever as a powerman, but the Roberts would have their power to keep air plants and lights and factories going. They had their supply of shots. They could defy the government for a time, and maybe they could force it to do the things that might save the world.

He stood up again. He unzipped his helmet and took off his suit. He walked out of the control room, down the stairs, and across the lawn toward the gate.

A little group of people waited beyond the gate, his Robert friends and Anne. Anne still there! Most of the others, Roberts and Norms alike, had gotten as far from the plant as they could. But his friends were there and Anne was waiting.

Kirk stood before the outer gate wearing only his slacks, shoes, and short-sleeved shirt. He held up both of his hands in an impulsive gesture. Then he opened the gate and walked out, unsuited and bareheaded, into the light of the sun as it lifted over the mountains. He heard Anne cry out, and then she was running toward him. He moved to meet her, the first sunlight warm and golden on his face.

Epilogue

With a power source and the shots that kept death from radiation at bay, the Roberts of New England now could hold out indefinitely. But it was not necessary for long.

The local radio and television stations flashed out the news. Networks in Normal country repeated it in frantic fear. Within the hour word had spread to all Robert country in North America, and Roberts went into action everywhere. Nearly all power plants were surrounded and blockaded, and several power lines were blown up. Within another hour, the President declared a national emergency. He called the Robert congressional leaders into emergency session with himself and his cabinet.

Twenty-four hours after the Roberts took over Plant V7 at Lake Dunmore, the President announced on nationwide TV that the AEC and NRC were dissolved. They were to be reconstituted at once, and the chairman and one half of the other members of each were to be Roberts. All the Robert demands were to be met.

Man had been headed on a course that would first have rended his civilization to shreds and then destroyed all men with increasing radiation. Man could now move again as one, all walls but the medical one removed, to a future that might yet be.

As for Anne and Kirk—little Adam was right. They named their first daughter Eve.

Manufactured by Amazon.ca
Bolton, ON

37847460R00152